Dreams Beyond the Shore

By Tamika Gibson

Blouse & Skirt Books

© Tamika Gibson 2017

First published in Kingston by Blouse & Skirt Books, 2017

Blouse & Skirt Books is an imprint of Blue Banyan Books

A CIP catalogue record of this book is available from the National Library of Jamaica.

ISBN 978-976-8267-06-1

Cover Design by Nucleus Creative

Blue Banyan Books
PO Box 5464
Liguanea PO
Kingston 6
Jamaica, W.I.

www.bluebanyanbooks.com

Thanks are due to CODE, The Burt Award for Caribbean Literature and the Bocas Literary Festival

ACKNOWLEDGMENTS

Infinite thanks to:

God, the giver of every good and perfect gift.

Antonio, my best friend and favourite critic.

My remarkable parents who paved the way.

My editor and publisher, Tanya,
for knowing exactly what this story needed.

To my grandparents, Vincent and Iona Joseph.

DREAMS BEYOND THE SHORE

Tamika Gibson

Chapter 1

CHELSEA

It's odd being mostly content as an onlooker to my own life, peering in at its major players and marvelling at their antics. There were so many moving parts in my manufactured world that most times I was a spectator on the outskirts, taking in the show. Times like now so? The entertainment level was spiking, and I was a mere observer to the unfolding production.

He leaned into the podium and gave the masses a slight pause, gravid with expectancy. He was mindful that if he kept them waiting too long, they'd take that as a sign of wavering. Worse, they would question his ability to persuade on the parliament floor. The people took to a man who could make his words dance.

"By the time my Cabinet is done with Trinidad and Tobago,"

he declared, "we will be the Silicon Valley of the West Indies!"

Horns ripped through the dense crowds and massive navy blue flags were hoisted toward the spotless sky. They feasted on the reverberating tassa, that seamless combination of brass cymbals and bass drums that awakened the senses. Homemade instruments and garish shouts formed a perfect storm, urging on this man, whom they hoped would be their next Prime Minister. Dr. Peter Marchand – my father – was in his element.

Most of the billowing flags bore an image of him, greying slightly at the temples, his jaw tight and his thumbs hooked into the front pockets of his expensive pants. His image on the bales of navy blue cloth was no statelier than in this moment, as he addressed the electorate.

"The last government was satisfied with the status quo. They felt that because we have natural gas ... and asphalt ... and oil ... they could just drain the coffers dry."

The bystanders shook their heads. I couldn't decipher if they were disgusted at the present government or ashamed of themselves for entrusting them with such power.

"Dem and dey damn cabal could get out! Ah say get out!" a heavy-set woman said, erupting from near the front of the makeshift stage, her blue head-tie wrapped so tightly it was likely leaving an imprint on her forehead. With that command, she shook her miniature flag with vigour, her chest trembling under the snug blue jersey.

"That time will soon be upon us," Daddy foretold, with a stiff, pointed finger. Then he detailed his plans, replete with punchy phrases.

No more nepotism.

A new era of transparency.

Accountability the likes of which this nation hasn't seen since the days of the venerable Dr. Eric Williams. Really, he had no business even uttering our first Prime Minister's name.

Each time he described something the crowd felt they'd never experienced, the commotion ensued. And then they quieted again, greedy for his next promise.

When we sensed the end of his speech, my mother and I unfolded from our chairs in tandem. She rose with the grace of a flamingo and straightened her tailored navy blue skirt suit. A diffident smile played on her expertly made-up face. If class itself had a muse, this woman would be it.

I brought my hair to rest over one shoulder, ignoring that every last curl had unravelled. Praying for some reprieve from the heat, I blew some air upwards at my face and fluffed my itchy dress so that my thighs could just stop sweating so much. My mother caught me and cut her eyes, so I returned to script. When I smoothed the skirt and started clapping vociferously, she seamed her lips in approval. She and I were on this silent seesaw of my action, and her equal and opposite reaction. I mostly riled my poor mother up just to get a laugh out of her. Though since the campaign had begun surging forward in earnest, laughs were scant around these parts.

Daddy's refrains were terse, but accelerating in tempo. This, the crescendo, was his favourite part. I clapped until my palms stung. The crowd interspersed his every proclamation with victorious shouts. Pandemonium gathered strength as it swelled through the throng of supporters like tempestuous Maracas waves.

"Tonight, we send them a message!" he declared.

"Those are your coffers!"

"This is your nation!"

"Tell them we want it back, now!"

My father's sophisticated wooing of the crowd ended with his indulging them in their ultimate desire for revelry.

Their chants rose like heat, engulfing the stadium. "We want it back now! We want it back now!"

A middle-aged man started to wine on a speaker box with arrhythmic gusto. His friend was not to be outdone, as he climbed atop some scaffolding, took off his jersey and swung it above his head, each swing resting on a beat of the music.

Some of Daddy's candidates for the various constituencies joined and raised their hands. Others gave my mother and me chaste kisses on the cheek. Though my face now hurt from smiling so hard for the night's duration, I loved my father too much to embarrass him. And so I suffered through yet another round of mannerly grins.

Christopher, our campaign manager, was barking into the microphone set attached to his head, seemingly on the verge of ripping out the paltry, loyal strands that had elected to still cling to his shiny scalp. His hands pointed every which way, giving directions. On a frustrated exhale, he pinched the sunken spot between his thin nose and tired eyes, and pointed my mother and me to the centre of the stage. Our family linked hands and waved at the crowd.

More torturous than all this hoopla though, was that my father would be the worst Prime Minister this country had ever seen. It's not that he planned on stealing the country's money.

His days of thievery and bribery were behind him. Or so he professed. It wasn't that the sins of his past would be exposed, rendering him a national mockery. His most damning secrets were buried in Woodbrook Cemetery with his partner from his old accounting firm, Mr. Lezama. I wasn't even necessarily concerned about him being corrupt. Daddy was too cultured to directly sully his hands, and would hide any incriminating trail far more successfully than his predecessors.

No, none of those things worried me.

He was just the most controlling person I knew. I fought like hell not to be like him. One night a long time ago, wearing my social consciousness like the insignia of my commencement from puberty, I'd called him a tyrant.

"Well dat is me self," he'd confirmed. And then, addressing me as his future Oxford graduate, he spread out my future before me. He touted my getting an LLB in England and then returning home to Trinidad. I would work with the Chief of Criminal Prosecutions before entering politics as one of the more genteel members of his Cabinet, albeit with a cemented reputation for taking crime seriously. My mother overheard all this from the kitchen, approval making her eyes shinier than the gleaming countertops over which she stood. I waited, all for naught, for either of them to really listen to me.

"I too sensitive for politics, Daddy," I said, my legs wrapped and swinging over the side of our living room couch. At five feet nine inches, my toes were almost swiping the ground. I munched on my most renowned indulgence, microwave popcorn, and prepared to persuade.

My father dismissed my self-assessment with a snort.

"Nonsense! No child ah mine could ever be too soft for politics. And dat writing ting I does hear you talking about, I really doh know 'bout all that."

'Dat writing ting' was his deprecating characterization of my most elusive goal, a seat in an incoming class of the Writers' Corner at Georgetown University. I'd learned about the highly selective programme from an interview of one of my favourite poets, Harriet Cummings. A native of Dominica, she'd described the experience as transcendent and transformative, and then wrapped it up in a lyrical metaphor that had, no doubt, convinced me that the programme was just as good as she'd declared. The Writers' Corner culminated with a creative thesis and a Bachelor of Arts/Master of Fine Arts dual degree. But I hid this aspiration from my parents, as if harbouring it, shielding it from their grasp somehow kept it alive and viable in the face of impossibility. They only knew I wanted to write. That I was partial to poetry. That I had no desire to continue as an indentured servant to this farce of a pristine first family.

My mother was perhaps even less thrilled about the idea than my father was, and so was quick to rally round him.

"Chelsea, sweetheart," she called from the kitchen, "you know I, for one, think you should do whatever you'll be good at. And I know you would make a very good Attorney General."

"But I want a job I enjoy going to everyday. I want to feel like I'm living my purpose." Even to my own ears, I sounded like a precocious millennial.

My father's caustic laugh had been telling. "Lydia, this child feel we on Oprah. Why you think it call work? Look here eh girl."

The empathetic look my mother gave me was mixed with

mild disappointment.

"Ms. Lady, I done talk eh! Keep dem story book ting out my house," my father said.

When he addressed me by that moniker, it usually meant that my father was done talking, as evidenced by the way our conversation ended just then. A cutting response formed and died in my mouth. It wasn't worth the effort that night. I would have much bigger battles to fight in the subsequent months.

Now, waving at the thick crowds of people, I envisioned myself, ten years in the future, standing on a rickety, plywood stage just like this one, built of power, privilege and lies. My mother tightened her grip on my left hand and the three of us saluted the crowd one last time. With my tired arm suspended in the air, I watched myself start to suffocate under the weight of reality. I pried her fingers off, making a playful show of the fact that she had me in the signature vice grip that belonged only to mothers. And then a certainty inflated within me, spreading through my limbs. Surely, it was only a matter of time until I grew weary of being an eyewitness to this next phase of my life, and devised a plan to weasel out of the path that had been so neatly prepared for me.

* * *

I lowered my head as security manoeuvred me backstage and to the entrance of the stadium, past the technicians and mic men. As the campaign hadn't started too long ago, and this was my father's inaugural attempt at leading the nation, I was still getting used to being shuffled from one venue to the next.

The security thing in particular was both novel and irksome. My clutch vibrated with what I was certain was a text from my best friend, who'd promised to watch the live stream of the rally.

I offered a kind smile to the burly man keeping step beside me.

"I'll be okay to walk to the car from here, Mr. Carrington."

He glanced around with shifty eyes, uncertain about letting me out of his sight. Contractually speaking, he wasn't supposed to leave my side just yet. But my night shift as 'dutiful daughter' had ended, and I needed to breathe.

"Really, Mr. Carrington. I could practically see the car," I pushed. "Plus, I sure Daddy needs you more than I do. You know how those crowds like to bum-rush him as soon as he's done with his address."

Mr. Carrington grunted and his expression remained surly. But he looked around again, started walking backwards and then pivoted to return to the stadium. I checked my phone, cracking up at the text.

> DAHLIA: Well yes allyuh, dat is Prime Minister for yuh money.

> ME: I know right. Though I sure you just saying that cause you find he cute.

> DAHLIA: Steups, Uncle Peter know he's a looker.

> ME: Break the chains of delusion, Lord. Touch her eyes in a special way.

DAHLIA: LOL. Miss you, friend.

ME: Naturally. I miss your pineapple upside down cake.

DAHLIA: Oh, haul yuh tail, yuh li'l ingrate.

She had me laughing hard. Dahlia was in Washington, DC now, having moved with her mother last year. We'd been friends since Ms. Bruce's standard one class in primary school, prattling so much that she had separated us about four times during the term before threatening to tell our parents about our disruptive behaviour at the next PTA meeting. It was usually when we spoke that I realized how terribly I missed her. My phone lit up in my hand again.

DAHLIA: Mammy ask me if I texting her favourite daughter. If you see her peepin over meh shoulder with she fast self.

ME: Don't be jealous, sis. And don't terrorize Mummy Sandrine either.

DAHLIA: Traitor! Still, I can't wait for you to move up here. Then you could entertain her all you want.

ME: How I reaching? Like you eh see how Mummy almost cut off my circulation on that stage. I swear the woman was going and snap my wrist.

DAHLIA: I'll bet money yuh find a way. You feel is now I know you? Like you forget that scheme you concoct when Beyoncé was down here.

ME: I don't know what you're talking about.

DAHLIA: Mmhmm, sure. One minute you bawlin how Uncle Peter will kill yuh, next minute you orchestrating elaborate fake sleepover by my house, sweet-talking dem parents ah yours. Tired tell you yuh have to teach me how yuh does do it.

Dahlia had suggested that that aspect of my personality had some horoscopic significance but astrology was too abstract for my taste, and my typical response had been to wave her off. Unsure of how to respond, my hand stilled. My thumb hovered uncertainly before eventually doing a tango over the buttons.

DAHLIA: Chelsea Marchand silent? I ent worried though. Uncle Peter will get the shock of his life when the time reach for you to leave. And he's a Taurus too? Dem real resistant to change.

ME: Well yuh know me, inducing heart attacks since the year 2000.

DAHLIA: Anyhow, how come meh boy Carlisle ent text us yet? Ent you say you buying a new phone for him?

ME: We got him one for his birthday. He say he eh able. How everything only sliding away from him when he touch it. He givin meh one cut eye here. Ah gone.

"You don't have no boyfriend so you have to be talking to Dahlia, the way you grinning so," Carlisle said as I reached the car. He had the door already open even though I'd told him countless times it wasn't necessary.

"She ask for you."

"Tell her I hope she not pickin' up no damn foreign accent eh, we don't want no part ah dat nonsense," he said, ensconcing me in the back seat.

"Not she. She still talking more Trini than you and me put together."

Carlisle had come barrelling into the Marchand family a few days before my tenth birthday. He'd actually been Mr. Lezama's driver, back when he and my father worked together. His discretion was impeccable, so by the time Mr. Lezama was murdered, Carlisle had already proven he was worth his weight in gold. Besides, Carlisle had been witness to entirely too much when it came to my father and Mr. Lezama. If Daddy hadn't made him an asset, he could have easily become a liability. Over the years, he had come to be just as loyal to Daddy as he'd been to his former boss, if not more so. His abrasiveness only added to his charm. At the inception of the campaign, Christopher had suggested that my father hire a driver who was decidedly more ... refined. Daddy had warned him that if that asinine, cow dung of a suggestion was indicative of his campaigning abilities, he might as well not return to work for him the following day. That was the last I'd heard of that.

I sank into the leather seat of the car, my head falling against the window's edge. I loosened the belt on my dress and hitched my skirt tail up to my knees. My parents had lingered behind to hug supporters and kiss their babies. Some of the music from the stadium had died down, but even from a distance, I could still hear strains from the artist commissioned for this year's election. It was an infectious ragga soca chant that even I hummed unconsciously.

Doh stress, just vote the Alliance for National Progress.

On the days I felt like a chatterbox, Carlisle engaged me without hesitation. So I appreciated this same keenness tonight, which caused him to leave me to my own thoughts. Time droned as I stared out into the black night, my mind warring. When I overheard my parents approaching the car, I bemoaned that I couldn't have a few more minutes alone with the black sky, the hum of the air conditioning and a silent Carlisle. With my mother wearing a giddy look and my father sporting reserved confidence, we sped away into the humid night.

"That was really impressive, Daddy."

"You find so, eh?" he asked.

"Mhmm, very Prime Ministerial," I said, leaning my head back against the seat. Strangely, he appreciated my feedback on his performances, so I never spared either my critique or praise.

"I like how you tell them to assume responsibility for their government. That they in control. I wonder if they know who they dealing with."

Instantly, he glared at me. His fingers began tapping his knee.

"Well, maybe it's high time for your father's style of leadership," my mother said.

"Trinidad's very own Jean-Claude Duvalier. Yeah, Mummy – I'm sure the people just can't wait."

"Goodness gracious, Chelsea, why you dramatic so?" she questioned in a huff. "What so wrong with a man who doesn't pussyfoot around doing the dirty work? Anyway, whatever we're doing is paying dividends. There was a poll in yesterday's papers. The party looking plenty better than last month."

Daddy's eyes avoided mine, but the restraint in his voice demonstrated his attempt to appease me. "This is a country I'll be running, Chelsea. Not a parlour selling dinner mints and salt prunes. You think America became so prosperous by being honourable and virtuous?"

He steupsed, his jaw tense.

The farther we cruised down the highway, the more relief ballooned in my chest. We were headed to a town hall meeting in Gasparillo. To my father's chagrin, Christopher had cautioned that the ANP needed to do more outreach further south than Couva. If the party was to be called the Alliance for National Progress, it had to espouse development as it was interpreted by different pockets of the population. Country people, in particular, could not be ignored. And my father was more than adept at forgetting that he was raised in the country.

"They don't have very complex demands, you know," Christopher had argued. He'd seemed sure of his words and had my father's ear.

"And they are loyalists. Once you hook them, you have their children loyalty and their grandchildren own too. And you grow up in South? Man, that self is fertile ground for a couple seats down that side."

That advice Daddy had heeded, as his plans involved a political dynasty spanning decades, with me as one of the minstrels. And so we'd taken a few trips down South, going as far as Point Fortin and Los Iros. Daddy would leave his suit jacket in the car and roll up his shirtsleeves to appear as a man of the people. With them, he'd use words with broken off ends and phrases with age-old significance. My mother called it 'rootsy', in an attempt to make this version of her husband more palatable for her. For the elderly in the crowd, he'd conjure up images of a simpler yesteryear with farmlands stretching for miles and a flourishing agricultural sector. And almost in the same breath, he'd lure the young with guarantees of more subsidies for non-traditional courses of education.

"I think I too tired for the town hall. I just wanna go by Gramma and stay down South tonight," I told them both.

"Chelsea, how much times I hadda tell you I don't want you staying down there with all dem bloody warahoon running 'round?" Daddy demanded, his finesse slipping.

Carlisle cleared his throat and scratched the side of his neck. My mother clucked delicately before pinching her lips together. This whole exhausting exchange was a circus of trite facial expressions and corresponding sounds.

"And Christopher done talk to us about the whole family attending all the events," he added, this time with a bit less volume.

I tempered myself as much as I could before responding. "You not running to be the President of the United States,

Daddy. You don't need to prance around with your wholesome first family like an accessory."

Daddy snorted. "I know you not holding up America as some political paragon." He peered out the window and continued speaking. "Even when you're running to be the leader of the free world, you use whatever weaponry is at your disposal."

"Honey, you gonna make Carlisle drive back down here so early tomorrow to pick you up?" Mummy interjected softly. "Remember, you have to sign up for maths lessons in the morning."

"I doh mind, you know, Mrs. M," Carlisle said. "Is drive you and the boss-man does pay meh to drive."

Carlisle caught my mother's gaze in the rear-view mirror. His easy acquiescence didn't thrill her.

"Hear what. Allyuh go and show these Gasparillo people what a real Prime Minister look like. Say you sorry your daughter couldn't make it, but she hadda go lessons early in the morning."

My father looked intrigued by the suggestion. Encouraged, Carlisle became more insistent in his advocacy.

"Tell them dat is the difference between you and that next man who running. I does can't even remember the man name good self."

"Down to your first-born girl child know the meaning of getting up early and putting in a hard day's work," I added, widening the crack Carlisle had made in Daddy's defences. "Your commitment to education starts under your own roof. Can Roger Pierre really say the same? Come on, Daddy, that's the perfect segue to talk about the raise for teachers."

He became pensive, rehearsing this new addition to his spiel, turning my words over in his brain.

Seeing my father's resolve weakening, I threw myself on him, wrapping my arms around his back as much as the car seat allowed.

"Thanks, Daddy!"

"Save your thanks," he grumbled. "Doh feel I eh know you and Carlisle in alliance."

Just then, we pulled up to the Gasparillo Community Centre. There was only a fraction of the fanfare we'd just experienced at the stadium, but the air was tinged with anticipation just the same. I saw Christopher at the top of the stairs, waving the two security guards towards the car. It was a wonder he gave Carlisle talk for his reckless driving, because he always arrived at the venues before we did.

"Not a minute late for class in the morning eh, Ms. Lady," my father warned, his hand on the door handle. As thankful as I was to be leaving their presence, I welcomed my father's goodnight kiss to my forehead. When my mother held me, I breathed in her signature perfume, crisp with a slight flowery-sweetness underneath.

Raucous applause erupted as Christopher ushered them up the stairs and into the building. I was sure Daddy hardly considered the structure suitable for a future Prime Minister, with its aging or missing louvers in random places, and seemingly on the verge of collapse. But the smile he plastered on his face as he stood at the doorway was dazzling all the same. Carlisle pulled away from the pavement and headed further down country.

"Thanks, Carlisle," I said, planting a kiss on his wrinkled cheek.

"So you feel I do that for you? I just tryin' to get some of whatever it is your grandmother have in that pot tonight. Leh we go down the road quick before dat cousin ah yours eat all. You know how she damn lickerish already."

Chapter 2

CHELSEA

The building went by a simple, imperial name. The Clark Centre. The stately, white structure was wrapped with towering wrought iron that enhanced its grandeur and exuded impermeability. It stood in stark contrast to the flat, brightly-painted houses flanking it from a distance. The precisely manicured lawn proved impervious to the unyielding sun; the grass remained the same bright green, with a constant, artificial finish. The Centre was located in the heart of St. Augustine and had about fifteen classrooms and a large, echoey auditorium. The owners had built it exclusively for lessons and prep courses, for everything from the Secondary Entrance Assessment to a full range of CAPE subjects. Augmenting its mysticism was the incessant talk about how The Centre preserved its calibre. From what I'd heard, the screening process for teachers included extensive checks into their educational backgrounds and qualifications, and pokes and prods into their personal lives for good measure.

Carlisle dropped me off just as I was balling up the wax paper from my two doubles and cleaning the remains from my fingers. He told me that he was taking his mother to the San Juan market and would return to collect me around noon. Compared to some of the spruced girls I spotted as I headed into the building, I might as well have accompanied him to the market with a Styrofoam cooler filled with king fish. I was wearing my favourite pair of washed out skinny jeans, and a white jersey, fitted over hips that were only now stubbornly coming in. My hair was tied up in a ballerina bun atop my head, a black headband restraining some unruly strands.

Now that we were in the thick of the August holidays, the building was teeming with students registering for classes and buzzing with the excitement of friends who hadn't seen one another since the school term ended last month. The inside of The Centre was a stiff, starchy white. It was sterile and modern, outfitted with monitors guiding the students to the appropriate registration lines. I saw some familiar faces from my year and smiled reservedly at a few. While I wouldn't readily claim the label 'anti-social', I'd mostly kept to myself since Dahlia left. I spotted the line for CAPE maths at the far end of the open waiting area and was relieved to see only one person ahead of me. She was a stocky, panicky girl, asking the attendant about taking a course during the week. Amid hoping that her barrage of questions would end soon, I noticed a guy standing a few feet off, parallel to me. In between tapping away at his cell phone, he looked up at me with obvious contemplation. He was lean and even taller than I was, which was rare for fellas my age. When it dawned on me that he wasn't looking away, I gave a slight, tight-lipped smile, so as to not look like a prospective patient at the St. Ann's mental health hospital. He tipped his phone in acknowledgment of my silent greeting. And then as quickly as that transpired, he returned to the screen.

"Morning. What class you signing up for today?" the lady in front of me pressed.

"Sorry, morning. CAPE Maths – the Saturday morning session. I pre-registered online so you may have my name already."

I shifted my focus to him again, and realized he was openly staring now, taking his fill of me in a way that was simultaneously unnerving and exciting. While I'd found a few guys cute over the years, it was a rare day that I was actually attracted to someone. And well, my first and only kiss was an embarrassment to kisses. Darryl Seemungal, this cute dougla boy from my standard five class in primary school, had snuck it from me at the side of the school building. His mouth had probed over mine in a way that was more anticlimactic than it was rousing.

This sensation was different. His eyes wouldn't release mine, and that caused my breath to quicken and my hands became clammy.

"Chelsea Marchand?"

"Yes, yes, that's me," I answered distractedly, my gaze reluctantly bobbing back to the lady assisting me. She looked incensed.

The muttering under her breath was somewhat indistinct, but I nevertheless heard, "I sure your mother ent send you here to watch no man."

She offered a syrupy smile and quoted me a price for the classes. Unamused, I handed over my father's credit card.

"Your class is at the second door on the left," she said, pointing down the hall.

Past him. I wanted him to engage me, but in a brief flash of absurdity, I also wanted to make it easier for him to do so.

"Room 305. Your class starts at nine. And that teacher head eh screw on too good. She don't like when students running late, so take my schupid advice and hurry up."

I thanked her and took off in that direction. I slowed in front of him, opened the bag slung across my shoulder, and feigned great interest in looking through its meagre contents.

"I like your outfit," he said, pointing at me up and down with his phone.

I caught his humour quickly, noticing that we both wore a white jersey and jeans, though his rode a bit lower on his hips.

"Thanks," I said, "look like you were trying memorize it earlier."

He threw his head back and laughed hard, coaxing a small smile out of me. His teeth were white, aligned, perfection. His nose was spread slightly across darker, sepia skin and his hair was cut close to the scalp. As his mirth died down, his eyes zoned in on me, warm and unguarded, in a way that rooted me in place. I was too dazed by them. And I was even more awed by the way he seemed sure of himself, immediately distinguishing him from most of the other guys I knew.

"Alright, alright, you catch meh," he said, his face lacking any sign of discomfiture.

"Don't worry about it. It wasn't so bad that I can't consider it a compliment."

"I suppose I really should be signing up for subtlety lessons, right? Wonder if they offer those," he asked in jest, looking over to one of the monitors displaying the subject schedules for the day.

"You sure that'll help?" I asked, bemused at how this stranger emboldened me. Although I didn't have any experience in relationships, his obvious staring had diminished the viability of being coy. Not that I knew much about being flirtatious either.

"Nope. Wouldn't put money on it," he said with a lowered voice.

The smooth timbre of his voice unnerved me. But he had my smile building, stealing up the sides of my face like it couldn't help itself. I wasn't sure what to say next, but he spared me the task of seeking the appropriate words.

He held out his hand and said, "Kyron."

His handshake, like his voice, was firm and certain.

"Chelsea," I answered.

"I usually have more manners than I just displayed," he said.

He pointed to the round, oversized clock over the registration table, which read five minutes after nine. Ignoring its warning, I boldly absorbed his features in much the same way as he had done mine.

"I doh wanna make you late, Chelsea."

No one had ever spoken my name like that. I liked the way it rolled off his tongue, like he was testing it out and weighing its sound. At the same time, I bristled at his shooing me on to class like a little girl. It was too reminiscent of those committed to directing my life. That he was probably the most handsome guy I'd seen recently was irrelevant. I had no intention of overstaying my welcome in the conversation.

"Nice to meet you, Kyron."

* * *

KYRON

I not on rich girls at all. I couldn't deal with the pretensions. I rather have an average looking, down-to-earth girl, every day of the week. Twice on Sundays. So the last place I was looking to track anybody was here at The Centre. There was an intense, unsettling stench of money in this place. So it shocked me that she was able to hold my attention as long as she did.

At first, she just sparked my interest, like any pretty girl would. As she joined the line though, I paused the video playing on my phone. Even standing from afar, I sensed good, privileged living coming all through that girl's pores. But she wasn't done up like some of the other girls walking around. No full face of makeup. No towering heels. Just some simple black sandals. It was in observing the plainness of her outfit that I realized we were wearing the same thing, and chuckled to myself at the irony. By the time my gaze caught the thinness of her jersey, my curiosity had already morphed into something more. I was attracted to this girl. And she wasn't experienced enough to respond in a way that could hide her attraction to me.

Damn.

She had soft and smooth skin all over. Looked just like long-time brown-sugar fudge. And a nice little frame on her too. But when she enunciated her name, with that polished tilt, I was forced to gather myself and regain my senses.

"Chelsea."

A rich girl with a *stush* name to match said richness? With that little rasp in her voice? I would be asking for trouble if I went down that road.

Nah, I good.

I especially didn't need to be entertaining any girl with this exam right around the corner. I was uneasy just thinking about it. I was a poor multi-tasker and downright incapable of devoting myself to more than one thing at a time. That I had both football and these SAT's was more than enough. Shaking off her presence, I put my headphones back in and un-paused the video of last night's ANP rally.

This was a big election year and I had just turned voting age last month. Maimed by a disdain for party politics, I was ready to stain my finger for an administration that could really tap into the concerns of the people and regard their intellect. Especially the young people. I felt like we younger ones had denounced the tribalism of our parents and wanted leaders who weren't trying to empty the treasury. The influence of friends and family had no rightful place in my vote. His absence from most of my life aside, my father had taught me that my brain couldn't be used to its maximum potential while influenced and tainted by others' opinions.

"Always decide for yourself," was his mantra. "Even if you going an' follow me inside the belly ah hell. When the devil meet you, you need to stand up like man and say it was your bloody decision."

On the rare occasion that my father doled out a life lesson, it was done with a sphinx-like hardness in his eyes. A person of scant words, his strange, crass anecdotes remained lodged in my consciousness. But he had taken care of every need my mother and I ever had. If I had any allegiance at all in this world, he owned it. Politicians weren't entitled to the same.

Overall though, it seemed like they were gaining a bit more respect for the bravery of the electorate. The promises weren't as vacuous as I remembered from the last general election. And the usual picong, mamaguy and mud-slinging were outmatched by the candidates' pretence of sophistication. Peter Marchand in particular was more transparent than a drinking glass. Everything about his image was contrived, down to his buffed, wine-coloured shoes. But the only thing Trinis liked smoother than their rum was their leader. Plus, we had a habit of voting with bad-mind anyway. Not electing leaders we liked, just spiting and sending home the ones we didn't. And the last government had really make mas. So I could see him winning. He told the crowd how he'd scraped to earn every bit of success he had, from growing up poor in Gasparillo to getting a doctorate degree in accounting. The ideas he spoke of were impressive and seemed sensible financially. The crowd loved him. But there was something imperceptible about him that I couldn't place. Just as he invited his family to join him centre stage, I realized I was next in line. Slipping my phone into my back pocket, I ambled up to the table.

"Morning, good-looking," the lady greeted me, an open invitation behind her smile. She looked to be in her mid-twenties. I wasn't exactly opposed to being with a working-woman, but her forwardness was a turn-off after Chelsea's endearing bravado. I gave her a folded wad of bills to cover the six-week course and the exam fees. Her eyes and mouth widened slightly. She observed the irritation etched on my features, regained her composure and pursed her lips.

I wondered why Trinis found it so impossible to just mind their own damn business.

* * *

CHELSEA

I escaped the frigid building just after noon, welcoming the warmth that greeted me beyond its doors. My eyes caught a girl tapping her friend lightly on the arm. She whispered, "Aye, I see she on TV last night. I think that's Peter Marchand daughter, you know."

While practically everyone at my school knew who my father

was, the idea of strangers recognizing me remained alarming. The only thing worse than smiling at crowds for so long you could cut your jaw with a chisel, was becoming a specimen in a petri dish among your peers.

As I darted towards the pavement, I felt someone grab hold of my forearm.

"Like you trying to run away from meh," the guy said.

Was his name Andre? Andrew?

I offered him the brightest of forced smiles. "Hi darlin'. Nah man." Leaning into him, I gave a brief one-handed hug, only to have him trap me in his embrace a bit longer than anticipated. We were cursorily introduced to each other last month at a joint sports day for our schools. I had only seen him once after that, whatever his name was.

One of his friends called out to him as he passed by. "Lata, Andrew! We sweatin' on the ground tomorrow. Six o'clock." The friend inspected me and shot Andrew a look of approval. I remembered that Kyron's eyes had managed to roam over me in a way that was brazen without being lewd.

"Yeah, yeah," Andrew acknowledged, before his gaze returned to me.

"So when we going out, girl?" he asked.

I was hardly oblivious to the fact that Andrew was checkin' for me. I had hoped, though, that given the infrequency with which we saw each other, this moment wouldn't arise. Especially since I knew there were a few girls in my year that liked him. I'd once walked into class to find a few of them huddled in a corner by the window, fawning over him and some of his teammates from his football club. I found him good-looking; there was simply no denying that. He had rich brown skin and was well built. He was charismatic and charming and he made up in personality what he lacked in height.

"Going out? Andrew, you know we've only seen each other once or twice, right?" I asked.

He didn't look offended in the least. "Looking how you looking, you doh need more than that, you know."

My audible groan at his lame jab caused him to laugh in concession. I couldn't deny it, Andrew was cute.

He held out his hand, as if awaiting something. My brows hitched in confusion.

"Phone please," he said.

I entered the password on my phone and handed it over to him. He punched in a few numbers and then held my device up to me. When I realized that he'd saved his number under the title, 'Boyfriend', I shook my head and laughed at the audacity. Since he had the decency to look embarrassed, I was spared from disliking him.

"So the idea is, you know, for you to use that number if you want to."

Andrew looked plainly bashful now. He grabbed my left hand and held on.

"Alright, beautiful, I'll talk to you later. Hopefully," he said.

"Yeah, lata," I answered. I gave him a brief hug again and took off toward the car.

Carlisle had the radio turned to his favourite radio station, which played mostly ballads from the seventies. Dahlia had once asked how someone big and strapping like Carlisle could enjoy songs about star-crossed lovers and ill-fated romances. I didn't have an answer for her. Carlisle still, after all these years, proved enigmatic to me at times.

We headed towards home, navigating through the dense Saturday afternoon traffic that was customary in this part of town. Sidewalk shoppers hunched over to inspect vendors' spoils and haggle over prices. The air was overheated yet aromatic from the host of Chinese restaurants and roti shops bordering each side of the street. Half-naked mannequins donning off-brand apparel stood like ushers to aging storefronts.

A taxi driver summoned an older Hispanic-looking lady, ambling with the aid of an unfinished walking stick. "One Tanty, one! Come, we going down the road now-now." He beckoned with a desperate hand, luring her away from his competitors on the taxi stand.

"Doh rush meh, boy! You feel I young like you? After one time is a next." He ran across the street to prove his dedication. Bearing most of her weight, he helped her to the stand he'd left.

As I watched him cut in front the car, Carlisle reached for the radio dial. He silenced the music, leaving the atmosphere weighed down by a peculiar silence.

"So, England next year?" he asked.

"It look so," I replied.

"It look so? What you mean to tell me? You ent make up your mind yet?" he asked.

"Well you know me. Most times I'm content going along with the Peter Marchand show. And then others ..."

"Hmph, that switch does just turn on," he concluded. "I does hardly recognize you."

"I haven't decided yet though, Carlisle, to tell you the

truth. The one good thing in all of this is that they're paying for whatever tertiary education I want to pursue. That alone preventing me from feeling like Daddy holding me hostage with his demands."

Carlisle didn't respond, despite the patent contemplation in his eyes. This gave me further license to ramble.

"A big part of me despises the selfishness. They lived their lives, achieved their dreams, and now coming to entangle me in dey foolishness."

The traffic was at a standstill now, with drivers unleashing their frustration on their horns with abandon. Cutting into the silence without preamble, Carlisle spoke.

"Impostor."

"Impostor?" I asked.

Carlisle cleared his throat before answering me.

"He was uhm, he was a calypsonian from longtime. Dimanche Gras ... at the tents during the Carnival season ... he was in all the events. And when it wasn't Carnival time, he would do shows during the year for trade unions or Independence Day ..."

This offering of information, in this tone, was uncharacteristic. Carlisle was an obdurate, 'wrong-and-strong' type, adamant in the way he communicated. He hardly, if ever, spoke with hesitation. Now though, his voice held a hint of trepidation, as if his words were landmines and he desired to tread around them carefully so that he could preserve the conversation.

"He used to always perform with this little mask. Sometimes he would change the designs and patterns. Some would be fancy. Some ah dem were real plain and simple."

"Always with the mask on?" I asked.

"That man whole career, Chelsea. Every show. Every competition. He always had that mask on. He died a couple years ago. Never really used to give interviews and ting, you know. Outside of singing calypso, he was a kinda quiet man. But I used to watch him and come to my own conclusions."

"About what exactly?"

"Well, the whole persona," he said, gesticulating with his free hand. "He didn't move much on the stage with too much antics. Kinda like Shadow. Used to stand up still and just deliver the message."

I knew Shadow well. He had some recent jumpy, hypnotic tunes that had gotten him far in competitions. A character himself, Shadow donned plain, black outfits, in keeping with his self-explanatory sobriquet.

"I was watching him on the Dimanche Gras stage one year. I don't remember much – think I was taking to the bottle a little too hard that night with some padnas ah mine."

"Well, they say drunk people make the best truth-tellers," I reasoned.

"Supposedly," Carlisle agreed, chuckling heartily. "That night he had on a black and silver mask. And I remember thinking how many of us go through this life like that, you know?"

He paused and then added, "Like you wearing a mask. Granted, the mask could change depending on the occasion. Or who you around. But after a while that mask had become a part of him. He live his whole life wearing it. Never show he true self. Now he dead and gone and people still wondering who he really was."

"You think that's what they turning me into? A phony version of myself?"

That was a grossly unfair question because neither of my parents was forcing me to do their bidding. My father had given me an out, as my education would be paid for out of my Trust no matter which direction I took. When I was in form one, Daddy had sat me down and told me that with just a few papers, he was going to ensure that I wouldn't have to struggle while I was in school, as he had. The onus was now on me to decide if my parents' dream for me was one I wanted to adopt for myself.

"You know what, Carlisle, no need to answer that. I think we can all agree that my parents have good intentions."

"Doh get meh wrong eh. I respect Mr. M. And one thing for sure, he love he daughter bad. Ent no question about *that*. And your parents doing more for you than most of these good-for-nothing out here."

But?

"But listening to allyuh going back and forth these last couple of months here ..." he continued, again with unusual caginess, shaking his head this time around.

It wasn't necessary for him to finish his thought and he didn't attempt it. By then, we were pulling up in front of our sprawling split-level house. In a departure from his habit of heading back to his mother's in San Juan, Carlisle cut the engine and jumped out of the car. I followed him to the house, perplexed.

At the front door, he extended his hand for me to walk ahead, and pointed me in the direction of my father's office.

The stillness in the house signalled that my parents were still at the supermarket. I crossed the threshold of my father's office without observing anything amiss. His books on accounting, politics and philosophy were arranged neatly in their ordinary position on the expansive teak built-ins. His artefacts from his years of travel were in irritatingly proper order on his vintage mahogany desk. And the office smelled of the lemon-scented furniture polish I knew our housekeeper used in this room. Even his professional portrait, imperfections erased, was mounted above his leather chair, as usual.

"Carlisle, what going on?"

He didn't respond immediately. Instead, he walked inside, pointed to the massive desk and said, "Look in the top drawer."

My leaden footsteps dragged as I made my way farther into the room. Innumerable thoughts dashed through my brain as to what he was directing me to uncover. That Carlisle couldn't even bring himself to say what I was looking for was telling. I opened the top left drawer with unsteady hands.

Inside was a lot of familiar paperwork. The deeds to my parents' two properties were at the top. Under those were some bank account statements and hand-written notes from when they had met with their financial planner about two weeks ago. Just as I was about to ask Carlisle if this was some kind of joke, some heavy parchment paper caught my eye.

It was paperwork for the Trust that my father had set up for me when I turned twelve years old. But the stock of paper was different and I didn't recognize the font. I scanned the pages quickly, poised to probe Carlisle as to how he even knew that Daddy had done a new Trust. Before I had the opportunity to pose my question though, I recognized Carlisle's haphazard signature on the last page, as one of the witnesses to the four-page document. Much of its contents were the same, as I remembered. But then I stumbled across the last page, which rendered me a casualty of my father's merciless need to manipulate. Dread knifed through me, sure and relentless. Much of the language went over my head. But I was able to cipher through the dense legalese to understand that if I didn't plan on pursuing law, as he wanted, I would have to find some other way to fund myself through school.

Chapter 3

CHELSEA

As always, the stillness of my grandmother's village was a balm for my angst. Few cars travelled on this potholed street and the residents usually retreated inside when the sun sought cover. Early mornings were perhaps the loudest, with the din of radio stations turned all the way up. The elders in this village couldn't strain their ears too much while listening to their worship programmes and morning shows, charged with callers' lamentations over the state of the nation. I wasn't quite sure how they did it, but the neighbours remained unchanged as the world sped up around them and as the sounds of busyness grew louder. Something about that sameness made it easier for me to breathe here.

Carlisle told me he'd be taking a rest in the car until I was done with my visit, and reminded me to pack a bowl of whatever Gramma had cooked. The squeaking of the rusty gate betrayed my attempt to enter the front yard undetected. My grandmother refused to have oil applied to the hinges, adamant that she wanted to know when someone was coming in her place.

"Aye aye Chelsea, is you?"

"Goodnight, Neighbour Harold. How you doing?" I called, waving to him across the street. He sank low in his rocking chair, the side of his face illuminated only by the glow from the television in his living room. There weren't many streetlights on this narrow road. But the residents, most of whom had lived here since birth, didn't mind the darkness. If anything, I think they relished the way it reminded them of the years when they beat their clothes on washing boards down by the river.

"Well, you know how it is. Went by the doctor today and he say the pressure high. He give meh some tablet to take. He tell me to ease up on the meat."

"I hope you let him know that if meat was supposed to kill you that would have happened long time now," I said.

He rocked back in the chair on a laugh, wiping his hand underneath his stubbly beard. "I shoulda tell him that in truth. I will remember that for next time."

"And how Tanty Jean?" I asked. In this small village, chatting with Neighbour Harold without asking about his wife would be deemed impolite.

"Jean!" he shouted, tilting his head towards the front door.

"Jean!" he tried again. "I sure she in the toilet. She just done drink some Magnesia. Three days now she can't go off."

"Tell her I said 'goodnight'."

"Okay darling, we does see allyuh on the TV, you know. Your father is a big shot now. He doh even pass and check for us."

No, he'd begun foregoing that custom a long time ago. He was too busy mounting a stage every other night, promising an increase in old-age pension instead. In many ways, I was the tenuous connection between my father and this place from which he had come.

"I remember when that boy used to play cricket right in the road in front here," Neighbour Harold reminisced, pointing to the street, his crinkled finger not fully extending. "Even when he had grow up, sometimes he would pass and cut the bush in the back when it get high, give meh a little trim every now and then." He smiled fondly before slowly shaking his head. To people like him and many other elders in this area, the posturing, slick-talking candidate for Prime Minister was practically a foreigner. I wanted to tell Neighbour Harold that he shouldn't take it personally. That he probably wouldn't want much to do with the Peter Marchand of today anyway. That the man he was talking 'bout wouldn't even bat an eye at betraying his own child.

"I'll remind him to pass through," I said instead. "He so busy these days, Neighbour Harold. But he and Mummy will come down soon. I'll keep them in check."

"Alright darlin', I counting on you, eh. Tell your grandmother I have some orange in the back to give her. They sweet too bad."

"Okay, I will let her know. Night, Neighbour Harold. Give Tanty Jean a kiss for me."

As I climbed the short flight of red steps to my grandmother's front door, I recognized the words of one of her favourite hymns.

"When we all get to heaven, what a day of rejoicing that will be ..." she sang.

I parted the white curtains roughly an inch, and saw Eloise Marchand hobbling through the house, loaded down with her pan of smoking incense, brass bowl filled with water, and her bell. She was a woman on a mission, perspiration in the deep creases of her face. With heavy steps, she went to all the corners of the living room, seemingly on the verge of toppling over with each shuffle of her feet. She was a little slower than usual, but her voice, off-key as ever, still held its strength. This was her monthly ritual of providing a covering over the home. In each corner, she'd pour some water from the brass bowl, swing the incense pan around to let the smoke rise and encircle the area, and cry out fervently to her Almighty.

It had been almost a week since Carlisle had shown me to my father's office. For the last few nights, I'd engaged in a mix of venting to Dahlia and staring at the ceiling, envisioning my next move. Plotting. But I hadn't breathed a word of my discovery to my parents. Instead, I retreated here for fortification. Whenever I was unsure, irresolute, or even ambivalent, there was always a pull to this house – this solacing place of constants. The cream walls hadn't changed since I'd first seen them as a little girl; Gramma would just have them redone in the same shade every other Christmas. Checkered, black and white vinyl still lined the floors. And the eighty-two-year-old woman that I stood watching still didn't have a judgmental bone in her body. She didn't have an agenda other than to love and comfort.

"Chelsea, I old but I still have meh hearing. Close the door and stop letting in all that dew. Trying to get people sick inside here ..."

"Goodnight, Gramma," I said, shutting the old, rattling door. I kissed her cheek and went to the kitchen. I dished out some saltfish and dumplings from the worn pot on the stove and sat at the living room table. Gramma was a staunch believer in never turning down her pot, so whether it was rice and bhaji or pelau with plenty pigtail, friends and strangers alike could always find a hot meal here.

As I devoured my food, she continued singing. "When we all see Jesus, we will sing and shout the victory."

I knew most of her hymns from having spent so much time curled up on the worn couch in this living room. There was a cushion reserved especially for me, tattered at the centre. Largely, Gramma's songs told of being heaven-bound, and what people like her would do when they got there. She always seemed excited at the prospect. At her small Baptist church, Mount Sinai, she was called Mother Eloise. She anointed heads with warm coconut oil, slung babies low in her arms as they were being christened, and led sinners to the water's edge for baptism at the San Fernando King's Wharf. I had been to church with her a few times, though my parents didn't know that. They weren't fond of Gramma's 'simi-dimi', as they called it.

"Gramma girl, what really wrong with your son?" I asked, using my fork to cut into one of my dumplings with precision.

Her incense pan didn't cease its back and forth motion. My eyes smarted from the smoke. Focused on her task, Gramma didn't respond immediately. She took her time finishing up her hymn and the recitation of a Psalm. I almost thought she hadn't heard my question until she began to speak.

"I tired tell you I not getting involved in you and your father business. What is the problem now?"

I didn't answer her directly. "What you see me doing when I grow up, Gramma?"

She grasped the edge of the table and leaned on it, considering my question.

"Remember when you had recite that poem in church? You had on the green dress with the can-can. Ent you know the time I talking 'bout?"

I nodded, indicating my vague remembrance.

"Well, since that day I always see you doing some fancy business with words. From since you small, I used to put you to sit down in that corner right there," she said, pointing to the edge of her daybed. "And you would write until your father come to pick you up."

"What about being a lawyer?"

"Girl, doh bother with dat. Dat is the devil business. But then again, thing that the devil take, God does turn 'round and use it for He glory. So what to tell you? That is what you going and do?"

"What she want to do is become a nun, like the principal at her school," Shelly-Ann interrupted, waltzing into the living room, biting on her fingernails. Before I could swat her hand away, she grabbed my cup of juice and took a gulp.

"Better than having ah open passageway with free entrance, you don't think?" I shot back.

"Allyuh girls better stop that nonsense, you hear meh?"

"Yes, Gramma," we chorused. Shelly-Ann, though my older cousin, was akin to my disagreeable older sister. She was much shorter than my lanky frame and just a shade lighter than I was. She had thick legs and shapely hips, and had explained that she had spread that way after her first boyfriend. Strikingly attractive, she was also the spitting image of her mother who had passed away.

After my aunt died, my father had suggested a live-in nurse, but my grandmother almost had a conniption at that proposal. Gramma had reasoned that since Shelly-Ann was a nurse by profession, having her live with her was like killing two birds with a single stone. Although we weren't too far apart in age, Shelly-Ann was ready to put in house. She had a 'sweet-hand' just like Gramma's, cleaned this home from ceiling to grout, and stood in line to pay all the bills, from light to water. For that, I respected and appreciated her.

Raising trembling hands to the heavens, Gramma thanked God for us, her only two grandchildren. She retreated to her room to store her items while Shelly-Ann turned on the nightly news and positioned a puff at the end of the recliner. Gramma emerged from her bedroom with a bottle of Alcolado. With a great heave, she settled in her chair, grimacing as Shelly-Ann stretched her arthritic legs to place them in her lap. In the background, the news reporter narrated a gruesome killing, and Gramma broke from her wincing just long enough to beg her Papa God to put a hand on the country. Shelly-Ann started sapping Gramma's foot and the smell of the menthol rose and pierced the air, barely overpowering the lingering incense. This ritual too was germane to this home.

"Up to now you eh answer me. You asking me about what I seeing you do. The better question is what it is you want to do, meh chile?"

"I guess some fancy business with words like you just said," I answered, carrying my dishes to the sink. "But, Daddy don't wanna hear anything 'bout that." I set aside Carlisle's portion, covering the enamel bowl with some foil.

I returned to the living room and curled up in my spot against the couch's arm, my chin resting in the crook of my elbow.

"Well, when your father was small I had find he coulda go and learn some plumbing. Enough pipe buss in this place. He had watch me like a damn fool when I had say that though."

"I can't imagine Daddy as a plumber," I mused.

"Well, I can't imagine you as a lawyer. And both of allyuh own-way."

"But Gramma, look how much times you tell me I have to honour my mother and father. Like you forget about that?"

"And what about honouring your own self? Eh?" She sounded aghast.

"Plus, your father can't blame you if you doh wanna take direction from him. Lord knows he do enough in he day. When that evil had grab on to that boy so," she recalled, fisting her weak hand as much as possible as a faraway look crept into her eye, "I thought it woulda never let go ..."

It was rare to hear my grandmother mention my father's transgressions. Shame dimmed her eyes. Those same rheumy eyes that had grown darker and cloudier over the years, while still somehow glistening with pools of wisdom.

"You could go plant yam and dasheen and all. All that would be better than what that father ah yours do. And I not saying

Lydia doh have her nasty ways too, eh. But I tip my hat off to that woman. She alone could deal with that man."

"I want to go to school in the States. Write for a living."

"But it have pen and paper here. You can't write in Trinidad?"

"No, Gramma," Shelly-Ann explained. "She wants to do like a writing programme. I tell you this girl going and get married to her library card."

Gramma looked to me, seeking an explanation.

"It's this programme called the Writers' Corner. In Washington."

"Oh ho. Well I eh know what name so, but listen here, meh chile," Gramma urged. "I had my life and I live it. I wanted to suck starch mango by the basin, and that is what I do. When I close my eye and go meet my Maker you will still have your life. Do with it as you damn well please. You hear meh? Ask your father 'bout that. I sure he know."

I swallowed hard and rocked in place on the couch, hoping to fend off the anxiety I always felt when Gramma spoke of that time when she wouldn't be alive. Just the thought of it ignited tension in my chest. She'd always reassured that death was sweet in Jesus but it only angered me when she spoke like that. She, with her grey locks perpetually hidden beneath a cotton head-tie and old floral nightgown skimming her knees, was the embodiment of all that was uncomplicated about my life.

"Seriously though Chelsea, if Aunty Lydia and Uncle Peter not easing up on that iron grip you might just have to do your own thing. You practically a big woman now."

"Big oman where?" Gramma demanded, her mouth ajar. "Shelly-Ann, what kind ah schupidness you talking this hour?

Both of allyuh young still. Just remember that!"

"But Gramma, you just say – "

"I ent say nothing bout being no big oman!"

"And I does have to watch out for you Chelsea in particular," Gramma said to me. "You is a piece ah work when you ready."

Shelly-Ann nodded and stretched Gramma's foot against her lap. I, on the other hand, feigned innocence.

"Me, Gramma?"

"You self! Doh feel I eh know you have a mouth on you. And Shelly-Ann, watch how you let night come in and dem clothes still outside on the line. Dey will pass and thief meh ting dem."

"Like anybody want dem old bed sheet," Shelly-Ann grumbled as she walked toward the door.

Gramma leaned back and closed her eyes. But her silence was short-lived.

"Why you ent go and write?" Gramma asked.

"What you mean?"

"Ent you just say is write you want to write?" she said, cocking up an eye in my direction. "You want to go America. What is the problem? Ent it have plane? I ent going up in the sky in dem ting but you so could go."

"I have to take a certain exam to get into an American school. And at this stage, I sure Daddy not going to pay for it."

I'd been racking my brain trying to concoct a way out of this. My savings account had about five hundred dollars, but that couldn't make up the difference between my CAPE class and the SAT course. It had crossed my mind to tutor English to some of the younger students in my neighbourhood. There was no harm in my parents knowing, as long as they didn't uncover how I would ultimately use the money. But even then, it would take me a while to earn enough.

"I doh know why that man so wicked when he ready. With all that money he have sit down dey." Gramma scoffed. "And what about your mother?"

"Both of them in the same boat on this one, Gramma. And I think Mummy secretly wants me to meet some kind of upstanding Englishman to take good care of me. Like her husband takes care of her. I doh know."

"Yeah, I could see that," Gramma said, regarding me head-on now. "But you know how your mother stop. Your father was bound to get a woman like her to do what he doing now. He need that support."

While I certainly loved my mother, I was wary about becoming her, baffled by her contentment in standing by my father's side as he lived out his dreams. But most of all, I was frustrated that both of them had me teetering on this balance beam, on the verge of toppling over, my arms outstretched. How could I bear my own weight when their demands were tugging at me on each side?

My eyes switched focus and landed on the low table at the centre of the sitting area, where a stack of mail sat. An envelope peeked from beneath the rest, a familiar emblem stamped in the corner. I shifted the pile with my index finger, confirming my suspicion.

"Gramma, your pension cheque cash already?"

"Yeah, Shelly-Ann do it last week."

"And all the bills paid for the month, right?"

Her eyes were curious, gauging. "Well, dey ent cut off the

light. And the phone does still be ringing in meh ears."

I scrambled off the chair and headed to the kitchen, hearing Gramma's muttering in the background. "What trouble is dis?"

I checked the cupboards first and then the fridge. Both were stocked with the staples, looking like the first of the month had visited. When I returned to the living room, Gramma was waiting for me to explain. I hesitated, hating that I had to embroil her in this to wedge myself from under my father's thumb.

"Why you acting like you doh have a English tongue in your mouth?"

My words tumbled out in a rush. "If I asked you to borrow some money. You would tell Daddy?"

She didn't answer right away, just kept staring at me for a bit, curling her lips.

"I promise I'll pay you back, Gramma." I fought to not wring my hands. "It might take some time eh. But we have a good bit of primary school children by us. I could always give them English lessons."

"Well, I eh find is your father business what I do with my money," she said. "Go and get meh change purse from the wardrobe."

Chapter 4

KYRON

I had only stepped foot in the Walters Paper Company once. And with the way this place was making my blood crawl, it was one time too many. I was unprepared for the noxious smell of sulphur that curled around my face, practically smothering me. Even more, I was a stranger to the orchestra of industrial sounds that greeted us as we entered the mill. The press and winders hummed a raucous tune as we wound our way through the factory. Two paper rollers stood whirring in a corner. The beeps and drones of forklifts snaked out of the storage area and to the floor of the mill.

After all these years, it was still crazy to think that this belonged to him.

"Gary, where the mister?" my mother called out to a middle-aged man loading some pallets of paper.

"He in the back room," he answered, smiling indulgently at my mother. He then looked me up and down, realization dawning all over his face.

"Dat is young Walters?" he asked.

After a marked pause, my mother responded, "Yeah, this is my son, Kyron." She looked up at me with a fondness that would exasperate other fellas my age. Years of being paraded before family members had taught me to be polite. I offered Gary a courteous smile. He blinked rapidly and shook his head in disbelief.

"He have he father face, boy. He resemble him bad," he said.

"Yeah, everybody does say that. We going in the back, Gary."

My mother led the way past some enormous reams of paper before we eventually approached a small doorway to a shabby corner office. Rusty metal cabinets lined the walls, which were a dingy, stained grey. Exposed wire ran up and down the thick concrete poles. There was no ceiling in this room either. A single light bulb of questionable wattage hung from a dangling socket, suspended from the galvanize. Dusty binders, bursting with paper, were piled high on the floor. I saw my father, Grafton Walters, reclined in a beaten leather chair, reading the newspaper. When he sensed our presence, a wistful look shadowed his upturned face. In a fluid movement, he came around the small desk to greet my mother and kiss her forehead. Shorter than his commanding stature by several inches, she tittered under his touch like a wilting flower. She grasped his arms, which now held the side of her face. He cocked his head to the side and looked at her with steady eyes.

Just as I began to feel like I was imposing on their moment, my mother released him.

As far as my parents' relationship was concerned, I tried to stay out of big people business. And that was made easier by the fact that my mother was gracious enough to never speak of it. I'd never hear her utter an ill word against my father. She'd only told me that they were in love once, and that somewhere at the pinnacle of that love, I was conceived. When I'd asked her why I carried her surname – Grant – she'd explained that my father's absence during her pregnancy had left him guilt-ridden. He hadn't considered himself deserving of passing his name to me. He'd eventually come around close to my birth, but by then, felt remorseful that my mother had to endure the preceding nine months virtually alone. He had pressed her to give me her surname. She'd resisted that idea, having been raised in a traditional family that called for children taking the surname of their fathers. But she'd eventually caved under the weight of his insistence. I was Young Walters in genetics only. For all other purposes, I was Kyron Grant and I preferred it that way. Being here was setting me on edge. I didn't like coming face to face with what he was, who he was. It wasn't as easy to divorce ourselves from him when we were standing in his world.

With stiff arms, he reached out to hug me next. Uncertainty peppered our brief embrace, if you could call it that. We hadn't yet figured out 'us'. At least, I hadn't.

Several years ago, my father had set a wheel in motion to provide for us, and it didn't allow for much personal interaction with him. We had two credit cards in his name, which were reserved for emergencies. Anderson, one of his workers, dropped money off for us on the first Sunday of every month, and had been doing so for more than a decade. At this stage, Anderson was more like my mother's second son than a mere employee. He was a shrill-voiced guy, about twenty-five years old, with a gregarious sense of humour. The bitter running joke between Anderson and me was that I saw him more than I did his boss. Whenever he came to the house, he would come inside and chat for a bit, and my mother would ask him about work and demand that he eat something before he left.

After my mother retired medically unfit from her job at TTPost two years ago, my father started having groceries sent to the house every fortnight. My mother had no choice but to store away most of her pension monies in her credit union. And last month, a week after I passed my driving test, he had a Honda Civic delivered to the house. Despite my reservations about how little he was there for me in person – despite the things I didn't let myself think about – I was grateful for the way my father took care of my mother and me, and would continue to be even after I was old enough to make that my charge.

Neither my mother nor I knew why we were summoned here, but whatever the reason, our business needed to be over soon. I had no intention of running late for class. I felt my mother stiffen next to me before she opened her mouth to address my father.

"How you doing, Grafton?"

"You know how it is," he answered, resuming his seat and spreading his arms wide, inviting us to sit in the two chairs facing his.

"Well, we both know that's a lie. The details of your life are largely unknown to me. How come we here? You know, the first and only time Kyron came here was when he was nine."

"Didn't really want to hold no conversation over the phone."

My mother shot him a quizzical look.

"Nothing for you to fret about, Debra," he reassured smoothly.

"You know by saying that ... is now self she going and worry," I interjected.

He wiped his hands over his face, and reclined ever further in his chair, staring upwards.

"Just some small changes, Debra, doh watch meh like that. The business growing and I can't keep doing things like I've always done them."

I listened keenly, curious, wondering what it would be this time.

"From now on, Gary will be dropping off the money for you and Kyron."

"Everything okay with Anderson?" she asked, anxiety making her voice shrill.

"Yeah, he good. Taking some leave he say. The father living in New York and he not doing too well. As far as I understand, he want to spend some time with him up there."

My mother nodded, her countenance softened by empathy.

"I have to cancel the bank cards too. Switching banks by the end of the month. They just introduced some changes that not going to work well for my business accounts."

"Alright, that is not a problem. We hardly use those cards anyway, Grafton. And you know you provide more than enough."

In lieu of an answer, he dismissed my mother's assertion with the wave of a hand.

Against my better judgment, I considered arguing the point with him. He really did provide more than enough. In fact, he was tiptoeing on overcompensation.

"Ma right about that you know," I said.

"What about the hospice?" he asked, changing the subject. "I saw the chairman the other day and he was telling me that they need to redo the flooring in some of the rooms."

"Yeah, I surprised he even tell you about that. You know how proud he is. I think they might be doing a little curry-que fundraiser soon though, so they likely to raise enough money from that." My mother volunteered at a cancer hospice close to our house, convinced that her true calling in life was tending to the terminally ill.

I slumped in my chair, withdrawing from their conversation and checking my cell to see if I had any messages. My father insisted on helping out with the cost of the flooring while my modest mother attempted to dissuade him from undertaking the venture. It made sense that my father's conversations pivoted on money. He had a considerable amount of it at his disposal. I realized that we'd been sitting here for going on twenty minutes, going back and forth about how he was mending and patching different areas of our lives. Yet, not once had he asked my mother how she was doing. Or about my progress in school. How could he look at my mother like a starving man and not enquire as to her well-being? Then again, he'd wanted us to come here, after all these years, even though he could have easily sent this information in a text. That had to count for something. Of course, it could always be other things he was worried about.

"What you think, Kyron?" my mother asked.

"I think if my father wants to use his money to atone for his sin of abandoning us, you should allow him to do so," I said. This was getting old. No need to keep pretending when everybody sitting around this desk knew damn well what was really going on.

"Kyron!" she scolded. From the corner of my eye, I watched as my father grabbed the base of his neck.

"Ma, I have class at nine. We either have to leave now, or you have to get a ride with one of the new gophers."

"Gary can drop you back up the road, Debra ... if you need to stay and talk."

"No, no, Kyron going to drop me by the pharmacy," my mother said shakily. And with that, my father dismissed us with the resumed perusal of his Saturday morning newspapers.

* * *

Today, she wore some denim shorts and a black cotton vest. Her jet-black hair was in a low ponytail, resting between her shoulder blades. She was in a heated discussion with one of the women at the registration table.

"But it shows here that you've already paid for the maths classes. Read the policy on the monitor. Classes close after the first week of registration. No exceptions! You can't read?"

"Plenty better than you can dress, actually."

The woman deserved that one. With her burning orange

dress and neon green earrings and belt, she looked like a bunch of mandarins with the leaves still attached.

"Miss, I know what the policy says," Chelsea said, trying to mask her irritation. "I sure it's not too late to switch to the SAT course though. Think of it this way. This course is more expensive than the maths lessons. And that means more money for The Centre. Where's the harm in that?"

"Dem eh paying me enough for this nonsense nah," she said tonelessly. "Come, the SAT course will be fifteen hundred extra. You have that?"

Instead of waiting around to see whether or not she did, I strode down the hall, took one of the last seats left at the back of the room and focused as the class got underway. The teacher for the course was an overenthusiastic woman who looked to be about thirty. She'd introduced herself as Mrs. Cross. She enunciated the writing rules like her last breath depended on it, but had a kind face that belied her crisp and businesslike tone.

Chelsea was the last person to enter the class, and she did so to Mrs. Cross's disapproving tut. She offered her a sheepish, apologetic smile while she jotted her information down on the sign-in sheet. A jolt of unexpected happiness shot through me when she slid down the middle aisle and into the seat next to mine.

I looked at her profile from the corner of my eye, then tried to seem focused on my notepad until my eyes darted back in her direction. Apparently, I *hadn't* noticed everything about her when we met last week. Her long legs had that same buttery, honey tone like the rest of her. As if she sensed me staring, she tucked them under the chair. Other than that move, she didn't seem to be paying me any mind. In fact, she didn't even seem like she remembered our meeting last week, and something about that bothered me. For the two hours that followed, she focused on Mrs. Cross and took copious notes. And I tried, sometimes unsuccessfully, to keep my eyes off of her. Mrs. Cross was lecturing us about the ins and outs of sentence structure, going through her Power Point presentation on the dry-erase board.

I saw a small piece of ruled paper slide onto my textbook with neat cursive writing at the centre, and then I looked up to take in the wide grin across Chelsea's face. I looked back at the note.

I am the subject and you are the verb. If yuh leave meh, I'll just be a fragment. She prepping us for an exam or giving allyuh fellas lyrics?

I scrawled across it in my unruly writing and pressed the paper against her open palm so that she could see my reply.

Nah, yuh hadda keep it simple. Sweetness, you wanna modify the subject in meh sentence?

She skimmed it and her nose wrinkled. I barely held on to my laughter. She took to the almost filled piece of paper with a vengeance. This time, she just angled it towards me so I could glimpse her response.

You sound like an educated spranger.

I couldn't exactly disagree with her. Sweet talk wasn't my style. With both of the girls I'd dated, I had been direct and open. My first girlfriend was a neighbour that I'd known since we were children. At fifteen, getting together had seemed like the natural progression for our relationship. That had fizzled out almost before it got started; having your house located on the same acre of land wasn't enough of a commonality for anything lasting. My relationship with my recent ex-girlfriend, Daneen, had fared much better, even if it had taken me a bit longer to realize she wasn't really my type. I didn't scare easily, but that girl's intensity was something else. The texts were non-stop, usually demanding answers as to where I was and what I was doing. That kind of stress was for marriage, not form six.

I willed Chelsea to write me another note, but she was concentrating on taking down Mrs. Cross's assignment for next Saturday's class. Andrew, one of the guys from my club team, turned in our direction. He acknowledged me with a hitch of his chin and then winked at Chelsea. Andrew was a cool fella, if a little bit cocky. We lived in the same area in Trincity, and outside of club football, we used to sweat sometimes on the community field down the street from us. My only problem with him was that he ran his mouth a little too much. He had this slimy way about him, and could sweet-talk the prettiest of girls in a ruthless way that had the rest of us on the club team clowning him. He got through often though, so who were we to criticize?

Was she interested in someone like that?

I realized I was in no position to say. I didn't know a thing about Chelsea other than her first name. Her expression didn't betray her feelings towards him. She wasn't looking bashful the way most girls do when they're attracted to a guy, but she didn't exactly seem uninterested either. Her prim smile also wasn't telling.

What was this girl real scene?

Mrs. Cross's razor-sharp staccato jolted me, causing me to curse under my breath. Chelsea turned and looked at me, her eyes pinched. That disapproving look caused me to curse again, but this time to myself. It was only when her eyes softened and she smiled teasingly that I realized she hadn't taken poorly to my bad language after all. I couldn't understand how the little that I knew about this girl intrigued me with its contradiction. As she picked up her books and gave me a small wave, I found myself disappointed that I didn't know more about her, and decided, if only for the sake of curiosity, to rectify that.

* * *

CHELSEA

Mostly because Christopher had suggested it, our attendance at church had ramped up since the launch of the campaign. I knew the pastor was particularly proud of the frequency of our visits, because for the last six weeks straight, we were the lead topic of the church announcements. In a low and unnecessarily long drawl, he'd asked the parishioners to keep us in their prayer. He shook my father's hand with almost comical fervour after each service. And last week, pointing to us in our reserved seating in the second pew, he'd done the most laughable thing of all. With a satisfied bellow, he'd declared that his church was producing pillars for the community, who would bring light to dark places. That's when I was certain that he didn't know a thing about the Marchands.

Luckily, my parents had enough shame to call off the security in the Lord's house. That alone alleviated the feeling of being a showpiece, despite the existence of an underlying political agenda. I was only barely focusing on the message. Instead, I was repenting for using my parents' money to pay for a class that they didn't actually know I was taking. I was comforted by the notion that between my savings and the money remaining from Gramma's pension, I had just enough to make up for the difference in the cost of the classes, which just had to be a clear sign of a divine plan. Just as I was about to offer my prayerful thanks, my phone buzzed in the pocket of my dress. I became only more confused when I read the text.

> **632-1156: Is "hi" too generic to start a conversation?**

The number was unknown to me.

> **ME: May I ask who this is?**

> **632-1156: An educated spranger.**

My heart lurched in my chest and my phone suddenly felt hot to the touch. My parents were absorbed in either the benediction or the appearance of being deeply moved by it, so this chance to text with Kyron must have also been ordained.

> **ME: "Hi" works.**

632-1156: lol. What you up to?

ME: You don't think I should get to ask the first question?

632-1156: You're right. Ladies first. Fix up.

ME: How you get my number?

The dialogue bubbles appeared and then disappeared, evidencing his reservations about answering my question.

632-1156: I may have seen it on Mrs. Cross sign-in sheet when I was leaving class.

That made sense. I had left class as soon as it was dismissed, trying to evade Andrew for a bit longer. I didn't mind going out with him some time, but was trying to delay the inevitable for as long as I could.

ME: Hmm, you must real like me then, to go through all that maths.

632-1156: I wouldn't say all that just yet. It's more like your writing was so big, your number was all in meh face.

ME: Mhmm, sure.

632-1156: Your turn to answer my question now. You busy?

> ME: You could say so. Sunday morning reminder of how to evade brimstone and fire.

> 632-1156: Mmm, I'll pray for you.

> ME: Funny. Sounds like you have more exciting plans.

> 632-1156: That depends on perspective, I guess. About to take a Sunday sweat. Wanted to get you before I went on the field.

There were tingles going up and down my spine, straight down to the tips of my fingers. I had noticed Kyron stealing glimpses at me in class yesterday but I wasn't sure what those looks meant. It seemed he found me attractive but only from afar. He must have known that I was confused about his intentions, because his approach to me had been atypical. My mother caught me getting ready to text and motioned for me to get off the phone. I chewed on my bottom lip, pondering a fitting response to Kyron.

> 632-1156: Chelsea, doh hurt yuh head too much over there.

> ME: Trying not to. Trying to figure you out.

> 632-1156: Fair enough. It simple though. Yuh just different. And I figured since we'll be in class together for a bit...

Even though I didn't know anything about this guy, I

somehow knew that with this text, he was leaving it up to me. Allowing me the option of directing whatever this was without any immediate demands from him, despite the fact that we had already established that he found me attractive. There was a chivalry in his allowing me to choose, and my body warmed at that realization. In church of all places! A torrent of clashing feelings rose up swiftly within me. I was one part scared of what I was feeling and one part giddy that I was feeling it.

632-1156: We just talking, Chelsea, so stop tapping your finger on your nose like that. And save my number. Heading out the door. Lata.

I removed my finger from the tip of my nose as if I'd been stung.

Just talking.

If that meant friendship, Kyron was, undoubtedly, going to be the most interesting friend I'd ever had.

Chapter 5

CHELSEA

arlisle drove us down a familiar, winding street in Cascade, with palatial concrete houses flanking each side. We arrived at the dead-end, in front of the stately two-story home of Phillip and Monica Hinds, which was set far away from the pavement. Before Carlisle could even turn off the car, Aunty Monica was coming through her front door, welcoming us inside. The outside décor here was reminiscent of our own home, but far more well-to-do. An ivory balustrade spanned their massive porch, the driveway was lined with ornate brick pavers and the roof was a red Spanish tile. With all the clashing colours, the yard was on the brink of being cosquelle. To the left of the pathway in front of the home was a Zen garden with bamboo, a koi pond and a miniature Buddha statue. Never mind that Aunty Monica was a staunch Roman Catholic.

I was the first to greet Aunty Monica – the 'aunty' was used as a sign of respect. She and my mother were good friends, having met when they were working at a large insurance company on Wrightson Road. Mummy had left her executive position there to devote her attention to supporting Daddy with his career. Aunty Monica had stayed on and was now the CFO of the company. Their friendship had grown by leaps over the years, and now that the election was near, Daddy was finagling his way further into Uncle Hinds' good graces, as he was the Chief of Criminal Prosecutions. He'd been at the CCP's office forever, starting out as an inexperienced lawyer and working his way up.

"Afternoon, Aunty Monica," I said, kissing her on the cheek and withstanding her perusal.

"Look meh darling, Chelsea. Just getting more beautiful every time I see you. The boys musbe doh know what to do with themselves."

"They better know," Mummy piped up from beside me.

"I now see why your mother doesn't bring you here more often. You is a big lady now. She can't force you to come by your aunty."

"Oh gosh, Monica, you know how hard it does be to pass. And now, with Peter and the campaign. Time more scarce than ever."

"Doh mind your mother, eh. When you want to pass by your aunty, just tell Carlisle to bring you up the road," she said, linking hands with me and leading us into the house.

Aunty Monica was a cooking enthusiast with a penchant for being the consummate hostess. She and the housekeeper made quick work of setting the fare on the table. As conversation unfolded around the dining room, stewed peas, cacciatore chicken, chow mein and macaroni pie were brought out from the luxury kitchen in decorated serving dishes.

"You taking a sip after this, Peter?" Uncle Phillip asked my father.

"Well, if you drinking something I will take a glass. Can't let a man drink alone."

"That's what I like to hear, man. Just get a bottle of Privilege from the airport as I was coming back from this ballistics seminar. We could more than open it."

"When saying so, how work?" Daddy asked.

Uncle Phillip expelled a heavy sigh before going quiet. Daddy offered an appropriately empathetic nod, a product of Christopher's impeccable coaching. Uncle Hinds' office was facing harsh criticism stemming from a failure to prosecute the more influential players in the drug arena, the so-called 'big-fish'. Christopher had pressed Daddy to be versed on the inner workings of the CCP's office and their intelligence, so that he could create a concrete plan for what he'd dubbed, 'the indubitable scourge of the nation'. Christopher was adamant that the ANP might as well kiss the election goodbye if they planned on making a mess of that part of the campaign. The party was in the beginning stages of putting together its manifesto and as far as the fight against crime was concerned, the details were paltry, at best.

"Boy, I'll tell you this much. If you get through to run this country, your most important decision going to be the choice for Attorney General."

"And what about the current government? You think they turning a blind eye to all this transhipment?"

"I wouldn't be surprised. If the trade off is that they getting a cut, I could see how some of the bigwigs at the top could be pretending that none of it happening."

Daddy frowned. "Or even worse, acting like they don't know who's responsible for it."

Uncle Hinds answered with a small nod, his facial features sagging. I had a weighted feeling just looking at him. I couldn't imagine being burdened by the expectations of an entire nation. Daddy, on the other hand, looked thirsty for more information.

"So, you all have numbers? Statistics? How much product we actually talking here?"

"Well, you know I can't say much. But I can tell you this. It's not necessarily that more drugs passing through. Just the opposite actually."

Daddy looked surprised. As was I. There was seemingly endless talk about how the country was a trafficking conduit being raped by everyone from the Lebanese to the Colombians.

Uncle Phillip explained, "South American suppliers seem to be noticing the heavy policing in the Caribbean now. So as far as their shipments to Europe are concerned, many of them cutting out Trinidad altogether and sending dey ting straight West Africa."

"So, the flow of drugs actually decreasing?" Mummy asked, cutting into her macaroni pie.

Uncle Phillip nodded. "Them cartels and barons getting

more sophisticated, girl ... innovative. Now they have ways to get their ships from South America straight across the Atlantic without being detected. They don't need this country as much anymore."

Comprehension lit up my father's face.

"Oh, so demand higher than supply," Daddy concluded.

Uncle Phillip nodded and wiped his mouth with his napkin, the disgust and defeat evident on his face. I didn't blame him. It sounded like a battle incapable of being won.

"That's why things getting more gruesome," Mummy said.

"So this is the best conversation allyuh could come up with?" Aunty Monica scolded.

Uncle Phillip gave his wife a pacifying kiss on the cheek. "You're right, honey. Surely, we can find something lighter to talk about."

"Chelsea, you decide what you doing after school yet?" Aunty Monica asked.

"Well, you know how she always talking about this law thing in England," Daddy answered for me.

"What kind of law, darlin'?" Aunty Monica pressed. All eyes turned to me. And mine were turned to my father, expectantly, daggers compelling him to finish what he started. This was one of the few times I actually didn't mind his speaking in my stead. After all, this was his plan and he knew its intricacies best.

"Tell them, Chelsea," Daddy said, his eyes averted.

An odd noise rose in my throat and I fought the urge to snap. My lips moved rapidly as I solicited the right words to mask my agitation. When I was finally able to speak, my tone was careful and controlled.

"*If* Daddy manages to coax me into becoming a lawyer, I'd probably want to do prosecution more than anything else," I said. "Although, the way things have been going lately, I can't see myself going down that path. Might not be in the cards for me," I finished, holding my father's gaze steadily.

Peter Marchand actually had the nerve to look sheepish.

"You know much about the field?" Aunty Monica asked, reaching for the bowl of chow mein.

Only that I had no interest in it.

Aunty Monica didn't wait for my response. "Phillip, why you don't take on Chelsea as an intern before school start back for the new term? Now is the perfect time. She could do some filing here and there for the next couple of weeks."

"I don't see any problem with that at all. And we have a few big cases coming up. No time like now to dive in and see the practical side of things."

My mother perked up immediately and shimmied to the edge of her chair.

"Sounds perfect to me. I sure Carlisle wouldn't mind dropping you off at the office two or three days out of the week."

Without a flicker of emotion, Daddy said, "You really can't pass up an opportunity like this – to see first-hand the machine that is our criminal justice system. Even if you don't manage to go into law, I can't imagine that the experience wouldn't serve you in other careers as well."

I wanted to wipe the smug look off my father's face with Aunty Monica's fancy linen placemat. Instead, my lips thinned and set in a firm line.

"You know what, Uncle Phillip ... I would like that very

much. When can we start?"

* * *

KYRON

Chelsea's stomach rumbled like a volcano on the cusp of erupting, sparking an idea in my brain. Her eyes darted around wildly, only to realize that her growling belly had betrayed her to more than a few people. She caught me looking and held her head high, determined not to be embarrassed. Mrs. Cross dismissed the class and shouted her parting warnings as we filed out the door. She promised that she'd be picking up the pace in the coming weeks, and directed us to some practice exams online. I followed Chelsea out the room and when we got to the door, pulled gently on the strap of her dress.

When she turned to face me, I angled my head in the direction of the first-floor cafeteria. "I 'fraid what your belly will do you if you don't eat soon. Come, leh we go."

She winced and covered her face with her hands, but then she smiled so brightly that for a moment, my tongue caught on the roof of my mouth.

"Okay," she said. "Let me just text Carlisle and let him know."

"Tell him I won't keep you too long."

She gave a barely audible response, preoccupied with shooting off her text message. I told myself, almost convincingly, that this little lunch thing was just incidental. I was hungry, she was clearly starving, and there was hot food downstairs. But, I also wanted to figure her out. I watched as her fingers moved deftly over her phone, texting Carlisle, whoever that was. Chelsea was, unknowingly, chipping away at my previous assumptions of her. And yet still, my scepticism of her lingered. After she wrapped up on the phone, I led her downstairs to the cafeteria. With its brightly coloured chairs and tables, and the noise of rowdy students, the cafeteria wasn't anything fancy. But then again, this wasn't a date.

"Feeling for anything in particular?" I asked her. A few students jostled past us, pushing Chelsea closer to my side. Excitement spiralled through my chest. Her hair brushed my chin and I could almost taste the vanilla on her.

I'd decided on my order as soon as we came downstairs, giving me the opportunity to observe her. She tapped her finger on her nose again, seemingly torn between the options. Today, her hair was in a loose braid that hung over one of her shoulders. She had on a knee-length navy blue dress with thin straps over her shoulders.

So pretty.

"A burger should be fine," she finally said.

With my hand on her lower back, I steered her to the little deli section where they made sandwiches and burgers to order. I knew I wasn't imagining the way her skin prickled under my touch, and selfishly, I wanted to remain close to her so I could make her react like that again. For some reason, I wasn't the least bit surprised when she asked the lady behind the counter to top off her burger with plenty pepper. I paid for our orders and we found a table in a corner furthest away from the entrance.

"How you feeling about the class so far?" I asked.

She seemed to give it a lot of thought as she carefully peeled back the wrapper on her food.

"Well, I'm not exactly worried about the verbal section – I got two distinctions in English and Literature last year. But that maths is another story though. Since the first class coming up on Wednesday, I wondering if I should start my prayer and fasting from now."

My phone buzzed against my pants pocket and I scowled when I checked the incoming text. It was Daneen. Despite the fact that our relationship was no more, we were still pseudo-friends. That meant that while I'd made it clear to her that she no longer had a monopoly on my time, she still provided good company when I was in the mood to lime. I pushed the phone back in my pocket without answering and noticed that Chelsea was looking directly at me. If she had questions, she didn't voice them.

"Who's Carlisle?" I asked, taking a bite out of my gyro.

"Carlisle is our family driver. Has been since I was little," she answered.

"Oh, how long has your butler been working for you? Bidderman is his name, right?"

"Actually, our butler goes by a much less stereotypical name. His name is Desmond."

"What the hell?"

Her eyes twinkled and I realized she was pulling my leg, much like when she'd heard me cursing in class. I didn't give her wrong. I was being unfairly presumptuous and didn't take well to people doing the same to me.

"Okay, okay. I deserved that," I told her, my hands upheld in apology.

She was chuckling now, and I found myself wanting to do whatever I could to keep that smile on her face.

"Don't worry about it," she said. "It's been seventeen years and I'm still wondering if I've gotten used to my own life yet."

"By that look on your face, it sounds overwhelming."

She seemed to ponder that for a moment before offering an answer.

"Plenty times, it is. The expectations – you can never seem to keep up with it."

I could only imagine what that was like. I didn't think my father understood me well enough to have any demands of me. And my mother had never pushed me too hard. If anything, I was the one who had high expectations of my own self. I didn't plan on living off of my father's generosity for too much longer. This exam and football were my tickets out, and I was planning to capitalize on them.

"My best friend keeps me sane though," Chelsea continued. "She has a normal life that I envy sometimes."

"Who is she? Allyuh does go to school together?" I asked.

"Used to," Chelsea answered. "She moved to the States with her mother last year. She wants to go to Le Cordon Bleu. That girl could bake anything."

"She that good? I hope you not talking about dem little cupcake business, you know. With a box mix."

"Uhn uhn," she corrected, shaking her head. "Black cake, sweetbread, pone, sugar cake. The things that seem to take about a week to prepare. I don't know anybody else our age who even knows the first step to soaking fruits."

"You have brothers and sisters?" I asked.

"Nah, something about me made my parents decide that one was more than enough. Still trying to decide if that's a good thing or not."

"Mmm, well, that's one thing we have in common. My father has a small brood somewhere, but I'm my mother's only child. For the most part, it's just me and her."

Her nose crinkled and I saw her reaching to tap it before stopping abruptly.

I hadn't meant to make her hyperaware of that habit. I just hadn't been too successful in keeping my damn eyes off her. Even now, I caught every subtle movement. The way she shifted a bit in her seat, slight hesitation in her eyes.

"Go ahead and ask your question, Chels. It shows all over your face."

She pouted a bit. "Am I that transparent?"

"More like expressive," I shrugged. "That, and I have an insane sense of observation. Then again, you probably not helping."

"Mmm. What kinda relationship you and your mother have? As it's just the two of you, I mean."

"Well, we good for the most part. Whatever moral compass I do have came from her. And of course, I can't think of anything I wouldn't do for that woman."

"And what about your dad?"

It was rare for someone to ask me about my relationship with my father. That was a neatly folded and tucked away part of my life that I didn't pay much attention to, much less talk about. How did you explain to someone that you actively avoided a relationship with the man who provided for all your needs? I had to think about it, figure out how to answer her question without unbottling everything and scaring her off. Chelsea didn't look impatient though. She just sat there waiting, taking sips of her drink.

"I can't say he's been there much," I said, shrugging. "His money has though. And that's a hell of a lot more than so many fathers do."

She brushed some crumbs from the front of her blouse. Consumed by the task, she said distractedly, "And you clowning me about the fact that I have a driver. Remember, I know how much these classes cost. Rich boy."

I smirked at that one, yet understood her perspective. As far as she was concerned, there was no reason to think I was any different from someone like her.

"Nah, I ent no rich boy at all. My father money is he own. It doesn't feel like it belongs to our family because I can't really say that he's a part of it, you know?"

She nodded her understanding. "Yeah, I get that."

"I more think of it as me and my mother, and whatever he has, the two of us are just the benefactors."

"Makes sense," she said. We sat quietly for a little bit, as both of us finished our food. I didn't feel compelled to fill the space with conversation and she didn't rush to do that either.

"I don't trust money," she said without prelude.

I tilted my head to the side, a silent invitation for her to explain.

"It's the wrong type of fuel for ambition. It changes character. It's a possessive wretch."

I was sure she could read my disagreement on my forehead. "I think you givin' those blue bills too much credit. As far as I see it, money is just an amplifier. It doesn't change who a person is. It just augments character traits that were already there," I assured her.

She huffed softly. "Then that would mean that there are a lot of people in this world who are just evil down to the marrow of their bones."

I'd quicker believe that than blame some pieces of paper for man's ways. Granted, I firmly believed in the inherent good in people. But there was a foul underbelly to society that I was sure Chelsea knew very little of, and I tried to make damn sure didn't leave its scent on my mother and me.

"Personality wise, are you more like him or your mother?" she asked, returning to the subject.

"As far as my character goes, I'm nothing like my father," I said firmly, almost harshly, in a way that I thought, in retrospect, would scare her.

But all I saw in Chelsea's eyes was a prodding for me to continue.

"He's really detached. Doh betray his emotions. In fact, I'd go as far as saying he's borderline cold. It's hard to gauge his personality, even with the benefit of spending time with him. My height might be the only thing I got from him."

"But you respect him. I can hear it in your voice."

"Yeah. He runs a paper mill in Point Lisas even though his family was dirt poor. I talkin' 'latrine in the back of the house' poor. Wasn't really formally educated and didn't know nothing about business."

Her eyes sobered. I didn't speak about my father with anyone. So it was oddly comforting to be able to articulate, with this girl relatively unknown to me, how I truly felt about him.

"As far as I'm concerned, that man is a genius. He's been generous with the fruits of that genius. And though he tries to hide it, I know he adores the woman that gave birth to me. So yeah, he has my respect," I said, wiping the table with my napkin.

An easy silence fell between us again. My eyes travelled over her face, taking it in inch by inch. As usual, Chelsea didn't look self-conscious. She didn't look away from me. Instead, she held my gaze and the tiniest of smiles played on her lips. She had to know what she was doing, permitting me to study her features like this. And yet, there was an innocence to her too.

"You have a boyfriend?" I asked, not fully understanding my intentions.

She shook her head. I wasn't sure I believed that she wasn't in some kind of situation with someone.

"No admirers lurking around?"

"Well, you asked about a boyfriend. That I don't have. Admirers? I guess there might be one or two," she shrugged.

Her modesty had me cracking up.

"There are, most definitely, admirers. And trust me when I say it have more than your measly quote of one or two."

"Then why ask me the question?"

"Touché," I said.

"What about your parents? They have anything against the

boyfriend thing?"

"I think they'd encourage it if someone suitable came around."

There it was, the jarring reminder about who she was and from where she came. When girls started using words like suitable, that usually meant somebody of the same stock ... good pedigree ... family with name. I didn't think Chelsea would have a hard time finding that. Girls like her never did. I realized that we were both done with our food. I didn't mind lingering with her a bit longer, but I caught her glancing at her watch and figured she needed to remain on schedule for something.

"I can drop you wherever you need to be," I told her, only to see her eyebrows arch.

"If you don't mind," I clarified. "And if Carlisle doesn't mind."

"Thanks. But I'm starting a new internship today and it's kind of out of the way. Plus, you've already indulged me in my favourite pastime anyway. Eating."

"Mmm. You would never know that looking at you."

"Was that Kyron's attempt at flirting?" she asked playfully.

"I don't flirt."

I cleared our table and followed her up the stairs and out the building. Today was extremely hot and muggy, as it had been for several days. At the pavement sat a midnight blue Mercedes Benz, with an older, barrel-chested gentleman leaning against the side of it. I saw Chelsea motion to introduce me.

"Kyron, Carlisle," she pointed to him, unmistakable regard brimming her eyes. "Carlisle this is Kyron. He's ..."

"A friend," I finished for her. "I'm a friend. Nice to meet you,

Carlisle," I said, extending my hand. He grasped it and assessed me, his lids shrinking a bit. After a moment's pause, he smiled thinly.

"Good to meet you, Kyron. That's what allyuh young people calling it now? Friend?"

The fact that Chelsea didn't look sheepish about the insinuation, or move to correct it, did something to me that I couldn't articulate. She attempted to push him but he dodged her before her hand could connect with his shoulder. Then she jumped in the car and whispered, "Doh study he."

I stifled my laughter as best I could and closed her car door.

"Thanks for lunch," she said to me through the window. "I'll see you later."

Carlisle tipped his fingers in goodbye from the front seat and they sped off around the corner. It was only when the car disappeared from sight that I realized I was running about fifteen minutes late for training.

Chapter 6

KYRON

When you have a sadistic football coach like mine, you develop a habit of being earlier than on time. Coach Joseph was just that dreadful. So I couldn't recall the last time I was late for practice. The man had two pet peeves – lateness and laziness. His only benevolence was that he allowed you to choose your punishment. Laps or shuttles. I didn't mind my penance though. The extra time with Chelsea had been worth it, and I needed to burn off some of the anxious energy that lingered from our conversation. I had already set my bag on the stadium steps and started for the track to do my laps when I saw Coach hold up his hand.

"General Grant, pay what you owe me later. Line up with the fellas for now."

The strangeness of that request didn't elude me. It was only when I obeyed and joined my teammates on the field that I realized how charged the atmosphere was. Andrew must have read the quizzical look on my face because he shifted his gaze towards the back of the stadium steps and then back to me. Two men sat there, their eyes hidden behind their sporty sunglasses. They were dressed in all Nike gear, in the dark blue of Howard University. The school name was emblazoned on the front in bold white and red print. They each had clipboards in their hands. I blinked rapidly, hoping they wouldn't disappear when I reopened my eyes. In the background, I heard Coach Joseph introducing them as the two assistant coaches who'd flown in from Washington, DC the night before. He explained that we were going to play a practice match and warned us against trying to impress. He might as well have asked us to stop breathing. I knew, like me, many fellas on the team were trying to leave home.

I scanned the field and took in their reactions to the presence of the American coaches. Andrew swept his hand across his forehead but I knew it wasn't because of the heat. We were both going into Upper Six when the new school term started and we'd often spoken about getting scholarships and boarding the next plane out of Piarco. Dinel, who stood right next to him, was rubbing his hands together and jumping up and down in place, making a show of warming up. He was a skilful left-winger who wanted to play Major League Soccer. He knew that playing for a Division One school like Howard would be a good move, making that goal a lot more realistic.

My aspirations weren't as lofty. I mostly wanted a different experience from the one I had in Trinidad. And the more distance between my father and me, the better. I'd be perfectly content with a school that had a solid physics programme and a decent football team. Everything else was secondary. Coach Joseph was known for sending players to American colleges. Some of the guys would come back during their summer break and talk about all the travelling to different states and getting free team gear. The way they spoke about the crowds at the games, and the extra attention from the ladies ... quite frankly, I had been fascinated by their accounts. I knew there was a chance that I could get an academic scholarship but I wasn't looking to put all my eggs in the same basket.

Coach Joseph divided us into teams and handed us bibs with large numbers on the front. He explained that we were going to do three thirty-minute sessions, so that we could get a chance to play in various positions. I was naturally a centre-back, but given my speed and aerial ability, I doubled as a forward. This was going to be twice the work. I felt my muscles quiver and twitch and my mouth became dry. Promising to not psyche myself out of this opportunity, I commanded my body to go into auto-pilot and do what it knew how to do best.

Fifteen minutes into the first session, I noticed a few players trying to outdo others. Dinel especially was hogging the ball, but I knew how badly he wanted this. My ability to read the game well allowed me to settle quickly. At every break in play, I reminded myself of coach's directives.

Don't piss the ball away!
Be first to the second ball!
Organize your defence!

Coach had also warned me to be mindful of my movements when I didn't have the ball. I ran and played hard, telling myself that my body was trained to do this; that I had put in the time. By the time the sessions were completed, everyone was drenched, some bending over to catch their breath.

The assistant coaches left the bleachers for the field and introduced themselves. To think that so much of our hopes were wrapped up in these two men was mildly disconcerting. I shook off the thought, refusing to make room for any kind of admission that my future was at their mercy. They opened with the expected formalities. Mostly talk about how they wished they could take everyone but that it wasn't possible – the dreaded consolation speech. The taller one went on to say that there were a few players he was particularly impressed with, but that they typically pick a maximum of two.

I was jumpy all of a sudden, pressing my lips tight.

He called number one, Tristan, who was our goalie. We used to lime with him off and on. He pumped his fist and I could tell he was struggling to restrain a thankful shout.

After a short pause, he called Andrew's number, number six. I gave him a bounce of congratulations. There was no denying that he was a good right full-back. That fella could run like a gazelle all day. Nevertheless, the smile I gave him was weak and I swallowed hard. I needed to be alone.

We began to disassemble and then one of the coaches held up his hand, indicating he wasn't done speaking.

"We only planned on making two picks but there was another player that was excellent at reading the game. Decisive tackling. Anticipated the headers. He just had a commanding presence on the field."

He explained that one of the things they valued at Howard was versatility. That they just couldn't leave without this guy since he could play multiple positions. And then, they called number four.

My number.

* * *

By the time I parked my car in front of the house, it was well after seven o'clock. Other than the two fellas standing under a lamp pole, the street was bathed in silence. Andrew, Tristan and I had stayed after the match to speak with the coaches, all three of us wide-eyed and fidgeting like some fleckin' two-years-olds trying in vain to suppress our exhilaration. They'd told us about Howard's campus and programmes, apparently oblivious to the fact that they didn't need to sell us on anything. Our dreams had been practically handed to us on a golden platter. Before leaving, they'd offered suggestions for improving our game and building muscle as we prepped for the upcoming year. The talk ended with their sobering reminder that being picked was only half the battle, because we still needed to do well on the SATs. They both commended me for doing my classes so early in preparation for the October exam.

I hadn't called my mother after practice because I was eager to see her reaction in person. She probably wanted this more than I did, and had so often spoken about this moment. Her words rang with so much certainty I was convinced she'd spoken it into reality. I took the stairs two at a time, thinking of the best way to share the news with my mother.

I heard her, even before I saw her. My heart stilled in my chest. When I got to the door, I saw her collapsed in a ball at the foot of the television, bawling, her face to the floor. I dropped my bag and rushed to her, every last wire to my brain overheating. Lifting her pallid face, I found it soaked with tears and hot under my hands. My eyes shot around frantically, trying to figure out what the hell was going on or if someone was in the house. The panic in my chest rocked me as she gripped the front of my jersey and tried to catch her breath so that she could speak.

"Oh God," she sobbed.

"Ma, what going on?" I demanded. My stomach was rock hard.

I could tell that she was still struggling to get the words out, almost choking on her own cries.

"Dey didn't have to do him that! What dey do him that for?" She was wailing now.

A familiar image caught my eye on the television screen. In the top right hand corner was what looked like a passport photo of Anderson. The reporter, her mien a practiced balance of horror and sympathy, was telling of how parts of his chopped up body were found ablaze in his car, almost burnt beyond recognition.

* * *

CHELSEA

We sat in an old changing room, with lights that were glaringly bright and a few white plastic chairs scattered about. Christopher fiddled with his cuffs, his impatience apparent. My father tapped his pen on the table, looking at the young man across from him, Leon, with cutting scrutiny. Leon was the ANP's Youth Arm President, and the three men were going through some notes for tonight's Public Meeting at the St. James Recreational Centre. The Youth Arm was leading tonight's meeting and Leon was doing the main speech, to be followed by Daddy's keynote address. Despite the heavy showers punctuating the night, we heard the crowd building. The band was doing their sound check in the distance.

My mother's arm was draped over my chair and my head lay on her shoulder. A maths textbook sat in my lap and I balanced a pink and yellow highlighter in my right hand. The first maths class was tomorrow. As I was hardly a fan of the subject, I wanted to get a head start on the material. I was stuck at composite functions. I'd briefly contemplated the brash act of just bringing my 'Nailing the SAT' book and flaunting it in front of my parents, my tongue sticking out of my mouth in juvenile, nanny-nanny boo-boo fashion. But there was no need to open that can of worms just yet.

"Dr. Marchand, I think it would be better if I talk about government funding for university. The youths would be more receptive to that if they hear it coming from someone closer to their age."

"I agree," Christopher said, massaging his temples. "It's the best way to build that trust. They'll think he's one of them."

"Or they'll think he doesn't have the authority to make a promise like that. I can easily see that sounding too aspirational coming from Leon," I interjected. "They need to hear that from Daddy."

I uncapped one of my highlighters with my teeth and circled a problem I'd just solved, making a note to remember how I had gotten the answer in the first place. When my gaze met the men, I saw that they were looking to Daddy for the final say.

"I'm putting that in the second paragraph of my address. Let's move on."

And that they did, with Christopher checking off talking points from a list he'd painstakingly compiled, ensuring nothing was missed. Leon began practicing a section of his speech, mimicking the gestures he planned to make on stage. His delivery was painfully devoid of passion and conviction, and his uncertainty as to what he was doing came through his eyes. Christopher looked hopelessly bored at the delivery. I tore a page from my notebook and scribbled on it in large letters, before I held it up for Leon to read.

MORE AGGRESSIVE!

His volume increased and I flicked my thumb up in his direction. Returning to my textbook, I wondered if Kyron was good at maths. I had moved past composite functions only to bounce up against square coordinates. I could ask him for help tomorrow. Except that I wanted to be prepared for class and needed help. And I wanted to talk to him. We hadn't spoken since we had lunch after class on Saturday and I'd gone back and forth trying to remember if I'd said something wrong. On more than one occasion, I felt myself itching to text him, if only to say hello. I had hedged each time, thinking how bizarre it was that he'd handed over the reins to me and I was wavering as to how to manoeuvre them. He had introduced himself to Carlisle as my friend. And friends checked on each other when they didn't hear from the other person in a while. Satisfied with this excuse, I reached for my phone to send him a text.

> ME: Stranger.

It took him about five minutes to respond.

> KYRON: Hey, pretty girl.

Was it even physically possible to feel the joints in your knees weaken if you weren't standing? I could practically hear him speaking those words, softly, yet with conviction. Much like the way he looked at me. I wasn't sure I liked the effect that Kyron had on me. I saw him starting to type and set aside my textbook. My concentration had fizzled anyway. My father, mother and Leon were set to take the stage.

> KYRON: Chels, wanted to text you over the weekend but things real crazy on this side.

> ME: Something wrong?

KYRON: Wrong ent the half of it. One of my dad's workers get kill. He was more like a son to my mother than anything else. Only now she catching herself.

My jaw dropped at that disclosure.

ME: OMG Kyron, so sorry to hear that.

KYRON: Yeah. Dropped her off by the wake a little while there. Passing some time on the football field.

ME: How are you? Can't imagine how rough this must be for you too.

Although I knew we weren't very familiar with each other, somewhere inside me, I secretly hoped that he regarded me enough to tell me how he felt. It took him a while to respond, but eventually I saw the dialogue bubbles pop up on the screen.

KYRON: Still in a daze to be honest. Confused. Who would do this to him?

ME: Angry?

KYRON: Mad as hell.

Christopher tapped me on my shoulder and pointed towards the stage, where my mother had already headed. She assumed character as soon as she crossed the threshold, offering the crowd a dainty wave.

"Chris, if you think I going anywhere near that stage, me

and you going to fall out. We will roll on this floor before you make a puppet out of me tonight."

His brows collided. "You can't be serious, Chelsea. We spoke about this."

"You spoke, and I answered. I told you not tonight. I have to study." I deadpanned him, refusing to say another word.

Chris tipped his head back and released a deep sigh before regarding my father.

"Peter, come and talk to your daughter please. You not paying me enough for this." And then he traipsed out of the room, purpose in his gait, mumbling something almost indecipherable under his breath about children being just as bullheaded as their parents.

Daddy approached, standing over me where I sat on the white plastic chair. But I anticipated his reprimand.

"Chelsea, sweetheart, we have discussed our election strategy an untold number of times."

His tone was far more appeasing than his pointed gaze. "Contrasting our family with Roger Pierre's dysfunctional band of hooligans is one of the main goals of this campaign."

"I understand that –"

"Then why are you still sitting here?" he interjected, his jaw twitching.

I kept my voice soft and coaxing, counteracting his growing vehemence. "You know maths isn't my strong suit. That's why you have me doing these expensive lessons in the first place."

"Listen. Right now I don't want to hear about –"

"Daddy," I said, "it's either I stay off that stage when I have to study or you explain to people why the bright daughter you like to boast about so much failed maths."

He didn't respond, just curled his lips as he weighed his options. In the end, he just huffed, spun on his heels and went to face the crowd.

I took to my phone again.

> ME: Which football field?

> KYRON: Uhm, down the street from my house in Trincity. Close to the junction by the mall. Why?

Tonight's meeting was scheduled to last at least two hours. Carlisle had already met Kyron, and so I didn't necessarily have to concoct a lie if I wanted to see him. And I did want that. I didn't know how good I was at consolation, having been raised in a family whose expertise was wearing masks and preserving appearances, but maybe I could just sit with him for a while, and allow him to say anything he wanted, or nothing at all.

> KYRON: Chels ... I can practically hear you tapping your nose.

> ME: Don't leave. I'll be there in a bit.

I made quick work of talking Carlisle into driving me to the football field. I was dressed in a navy blue ANP jersey, white shorts and rolled down, hi-top Converse sneakers, managing to not look too out of place. A few guys were milling around when I got there. Some spared me a glance as I stepped to the edge of the grass, which was still damp from the rain. Kyron and another guy were juggling a ball, bouncing it off their chests and heads and whatever other adequate body surfaces they could find. When he looked up and saw me, an inscrutable expression clouded his face.

"Aright, that's me for the night dey, Dinel," he said to the guy, letting the ball roll off of his chest and giving Dinel the kind of handshake variation guys did.

"Aw haw. Sweet ting show up and is to hell with me. Aright General Grant, I see how you moving."

"Aye, have some manners boy."

"But, of course! Goodnight family," Dinel greeted me, his lips curling with mischief.

I waved at him and shook my head, watching as Kyron walked over to where I stood. The grass made a squishing sound beneath his feet, and that only highlighted how long it took for him to reach me in front of a small wooden bench at the side of the field. It didn't look like he'd left home to play football, as he wore some regular cargo pants and a red jersey. I faced him on the bench, curling one of my legs beneath me. He was only partially turned towards me. His eyes, usually bright and piercing, held traces of sadness. I began to feel nervous, unsure that I would know what to do with his emotions, if he would even entrust me with them in the first place.

"So I guess I know who you voting for," he said.

"Nah, still a paltry seventeen years old," I said, looking down at the ANP slogan over my right breast pocket. I caught Kyron's eyes following my gaze before looking away quickly. I didn't want to talk about my father and his band of merry men, so I changed the subject.

"How come you not at the wake with your mother?" I asked. He shook his head while speaking.

"Nah, that would make it too real. To hear people talk about Anderson like he really ent here, you know? He used to bring us money from my father. Every month without fail. Going past ten years. With that kinda history, somebody does come to be more like family."

My hand reached out to bridge the space between us and eased its way into his palm. He held it on his lap, looking consumed by his thoughts.

"He would stay and talk ... lime little bit ... tell us what was going on with my father."

"Sounds like he was the strongest connection you had with your dad. Must be hard to lose that too, in addition to a friend," I said.

Kyron nodded, his stare vacant.

"Makes me remember what you said when we were having lunch Saturday," he said, finally turning to face me. "Some people just have evil down to the marrow ah dey bones. The man who do him this will rot in a special part ah hell. On the slight off-chance they even find dat monster."

His expression went slack and I felt the tension, heavy and rolling off his body in waves. Kyron still hadn't let go of my hand but I wasn't sure he remembered he was holding it. I swallowed over the lump in my throat. Death had never visited my front door. Not once did it feel personal because it was always at least a degree removed from me. Much less a murder. Like the rest of the country, I'd easily come to accept the cycle of these cases. A news reporter would shove a mic in a mother's face as she wept on TV. Your belly would turn at the repulsive details. Some government official would condemn the act with strong language and offer a half-hearted pledge to find whomever was responsible. If it was high-profile, that person would likely be Uncle Hinds. But then, inevitably, the world would keep turning. We got up and went to work and school and fetes until the next one. Rinse and repeat. But seeing Kyron's drooping shoulders and the weariness in his eyes. Hearing him relay the details of someone's life and how they intertwined with his. This was a disruption to the cycle. It left me feeling useless. Kyron's friend, the details of his life, would soon boil down to another manila file that I would likely encounter at the CCP's office.

He started caressing my fingers absentmindedly, inciting goosebumps to steal up my arm, making me feel, even though he didn't intend it. I edged closer to him, until our arms were pressed together. I saw and felt when he exhaled, like he was trying to get the pain out of his body. It made my brain go haywire, scrambling for something to do to make it go away.

I only knew one person who could help. I took out my cell and called my grandmother. It wasn't so late that she wouldn't be up. Besides, despite all the lambasting she did of my father, I knew from Shelly-Ann that she watched every single rally and meeting. When Gramma answered the phone, she sounded irritated at the disturbance. I could hear Leon's shaky voice coming through the television in the background. Her gruff tone dissipated when she recognized it was me, and softened even further when I told her about Kyron. I didn't disclose much, only telling her I had a friend who was going through a family issue and needed some prayer for a good night's sleep because of all the studying he had to do. While I offered her the introduction, I kept my eyes on Kyron, and his were arrested by mine.

He took the phone.

"Goodnight Grams," he said, and a few seconds later, he closed his eyes. I shut my lids too, listening raptly as Gramma interceded on his behalf through the phone, with the same fervour that she did for her own grandchildren. Eventually, I heard Kyron opening up to Gramma about the murder, first in clipped sentences and then slightly more descriptively. Gramma had that effect; she could put anyone at ease.

"Yes, ma'am," he said a couple minutes later. I could practically hear the swift reproach, as that title had always been too stiff for her. "Sorry, yes Grams. You have a good night too."

When he came off the phone, Kyron gave a slow, disbelieving shake of his head, seemingly awed by the way Gramma had entreated for his sake. I knew that look, and so I felt the need to explain.

"Eloise is ... the source," I said, struggling to come up with more precise words. "That's the one person in my life who doesn't want anything from me. She only gives, she never takes. I try not to take for granted what I have in her." I really didn't know how else to describe that gem of a woman.

"Thanks for that, Chels." His voice caught a bit, and it seemed like he was a bit at a loss for the right words. I squeezed his hand, hoping I was adequately communicating to him that I didn't mind sharing such an important person to me. More than that, it moved me to see him receive her so well. He let go of my hand and I returned my cell phone to my pocket.

"That's what friends are for, not so?" I asked with a wink.

For the first time since I'd arrived at the field, he smiled that full, open, boyish smile. The one that I intuitively knew he didn't share often. The one that had my awareness of him rippling from all parts of my body, culminating in a wild fluttering in my belly.

As if he had a flash of remembrance, the look on his face morphed from sullen to reserved happiness, almost as if he felt guilty about what he was about to share.

"Some coaches came to see us play Saturday afternoon after we had lunch."

As Kyron told me about this opportunity to play football in the States, I was barely able to contain my excitement for him. I wondered if this was what it was like to have a boyfriend. To be made happier by his happiness. To want to stay in his presence if only for the sake of being there. To want to pull him close and kiss him right in the middle of his sentence.

Chapter 7

KYRON

I took a deep breath as I pulled up on the street in front of Anderson's home. Before we'd hung up, Ms. Eloise had told me that I had no right to call Anderson a friend if I couldn't even go in his mother's house and show my face at a time like this. Her gentle scolding had persuaded me. So right after I gave Chelsea the news about Howard, I headed there.

Cars littered the street and I was forced to park around the corner from the house. There were two large, white tents in the front yard. A few younger fellas were limin' in the road. Two of them wore the same uniform of choice – a dingy oversized jersey, sagging three-quarters, and a bandana hanging out the back pocket. The ones that weren't nursing a Guinness were taking turns with an Old Oak bottle. When I entered the yard, I found the mood inside the gate a bit more sombre, but hardly as grim as I had anticipated for people mourning their dead.

It seemed like the solemn portion of the night had ended, giving way to a more jovial atmosphere. Three older men sat in a corner of one of the tents, beating their shallow goatskin drums, their heads dipping and feet tapping in sync. A young girl joined in with a tambourine, and together they sang a version of an African spiritual, marked by local parlance, which intermingled with the reverberations of the drums. They were possessed by the beats they made and enwrapped in their own chants.

Boom… budum… Boom… budum… He gone along the road…

I threw out a general 'goodnight', and headed up the back steps leading to the kitchen. Ma was helping Anderson's mother prepare paper plates piled high with bake and buljol. After the surprise at my presence sunk in, Ma donned a proud smile and Anderson's mother lit up so brightly that I felt like an ass for even hesitating to come here in the first place. I kissed her cheek in greeting, then froze, scouring my mental rolodex for the most fitting thing to say. *Sorry for your loss*, seemed trite and *accept my condolences*, made me sound like a greying, sixty-year-old man. So instead, I asked her if I could help with carrying out the food.

"Thanks darling, but we should be good here," my mother said. "Let me just share out these cups of tea and then we could go." I stood at her side as she began pouring cocoa tea into Styrofoam cups and arranging them on a tray. Just then, I caught sight of my father having a discussion with Gary in the corner. Gary was animated. My father, on the other hand, stood ramrod straight with his arms crossed over his chest, his expression giving away nothing.

My mother caught the direction of my gaze and said softly, "Is he pay for all this, you know."

"That doesn't surprise me."

"Anderson mother watch me straight in my eye and say, 'you see that Grafton Walters? That man is a God-send'. How she can't believe Anderson was getting paid all that good money at the paper factory, and was just pissin' it away on rum. Yeah. And all dem years he passin' by us, I had tell that boy to put away a little change. But like stick had break in he ears."

My father caught me looking at him and hitched his chin in acknowledgment. I nodded in response. He didn't look like he was planning to come over, like a regular father would, which made my mother's hero worship even more undeserved, more irritating. So I told her I'd wait for her in the car.

The drive home was silent at first, Ma just humming the notes to a hymn that I'm sure had remained in her head from the wake.

"You could have said something to your father."

"This is very true, Ma," I responded. "Just as he could have said something to me."

"You could tell this hit him hard, you know. He would never say it of course."

"Really? Would have never guessed."

Ma wasn't usually this protective of my father. She would quicker hold her tongue when it came to him than come to his defence. I wondered about her impetus.

"He uhm, was talking to me tonight about ... about possibly getting back together."

My hands gripped the steering wheel as a barrage of emotions overcame me. Confusion was the most identifiable of them all. I had never heard my mother speak a word about any kind of permanent situation with my father. While it was obvious that he loved her, he had held her at bay since I was born. Eighteen years.

"He's done a lot for us, Kyron."

"Ma, just because I appreciate what he's given us doesn't mean I have to respect who he is."

"Can you really separate the two though?"

I didn't respond, just glanced at her profile, wondering if my mother understood the totality of who my father was. Pondering what it said about her if she did.

"He is not a bad man, you know."

"You trying to convince me or yuhself?"

Her lips curled inward.

"I never said he was, Ma. Though you can't really know someone's personality fully when they not there."

"He could be a little inhibited, eh. I eh saying no. I know he does mastah pull away from people." She paused then, as if contemplating how much she wanted to divulge.

"His uhm ... his parents was something else though. Repressed, passive-aggressive kinda people. Used to punish him and his brothers for expressing any kinda emotion. So, he grow up constrained. It doh mean he doh love you. Or me."

I understood that more than accepting my father for who he was, she was giving me some basis for understanding her decision on this whole thing. Was it even fair for me to have an opinion since I likely wouldn't be in the country soon anyway?

Luckily, I would be spared from knowing what a family would look like with my father in it. It's not that I harboured anything against him. It was more that he was just a mythical figure that kind of hovered in the background as a funding source. I wasn't pressed to reconfigure our relationship at this late stage. Would he expect me to call him 'Daddy'? Those words had never come out of my mouth when addressing him directly. That kind of attachment just wasn't there so I couldn't imagine how we were going to mutate into this prototypical nuclear family.

But my mother was getting older and I imagined she wanted companionship. I gave her credit for not doing that thing that some mothers did – make me some kind of strange version of her spouse. And I was man enough to understand her needing someone there in a more permanent sense, taking care of her. I just wasn't sure it should be him. But I couldn't go lecturing my mother when I didn't even have answers my own damn self.

"What you want me to say, Ma? Allyuh is big people who could handle allyuh stories."

She just nodded, seemingly content with my response. She proceeded to change the subject, asking me where I had been while she was at the wake. I told her about Chelsea and Ms. Eloise, and she listened absorbedly, hardly interjecting. When I told her about our little prayer session over the phone, she cocked her head and lifted a single eyebrow. I wasn't no big Christian eh, but the way Ms. Eloise went in for me over that phone, someone she had never even met ... with that intensity in her voice? It still had me shaken.

"Well, you know what they say. You could go to school but

you can't buy class. Chelsea doh sound like that Daneen one," my mother said. "I was always wary ah she. Coming up in my house with them tight pants stick up in she bottom like she going J'ouvert."

"Yeah, I remember how you used to be screwing up your face behind the girl back," I said, laughing.

"Why you don't ask her to go out?" she asked enthusiastically, as if there were simply no other reasonable alternative.

Honestly, I hadn't considered that a real possibility until tonight. I had no issue with compartmentalizing attraction. So when I met Chelsea two and a half weeks ago, it was easy to put her in a box, separate and apart from my physical reaction to her. But as I had gotten to know her, I found her to be more layered, and couldn't resist the intrigue of the contradictions in her personality. The way she made a caricature of her wealth one minute and then was frank about it the next. Under her finesse was a quick tongue; she was reserved without being standoffish; and behind her bantering was innocence. And tonight had shown that, more than anything else, she was compassionate. That quickly, she'd gotten under my skin.

"I doh know, Ma," I hedged, rubbing at my lips. "She cut from a different cloth. Real high society thing."

"So we is pauper? And even if we were, that have nothing to do with the heart of a person, Kyron. If I didn't know any better, I would say Kyron Grant feeling insecure for the first time in his born life."

More than anyone else, my mother knew that there wasn't a self-doubting bone in my body. I just wasn't built that way. My assertiveness had served me well as a young man growing up without the presence of a father. I made decisions without hesitation and didn't really give a damn what anyone thought about my convictions. Even the way I played football was characterized by my decisiveness, earning me the name 'General Grant' on the field. But I vacillated with Chelsea, certain that I wanted to be around her more, yet completely unsure of what I was doing with this girl.

By the time Wednesday morning rolled around, still dank with the remnants of the previous day's rain, I decided to put my reservations aside. We had our first maths class in a few hours, but I could already feel my anxiety at seeing her.

As I was about to head outside to cut the grass, I dialled Chelsea's number.

"Hello?" she sounded distracted.

I cleared my throat and said, "Hey, Chels. How you doing?"

"Good. By the hairdresser. I must really like you, to take a call while she's washing my hair. She givin' meh a cut-eye here."

"Oh, I didn't mean to interrupt ..."

"Nah, is no problem. What's up?"

"You coming to class today?"

"Yeah, I should be done here in like an hour and then I heading home."

"Okay. You have a ride?"

Of course she have a ride you big dummy, ent you meet him already?

I heard her chuckling, which, in turn, made me laugh at my own self and rub at my forehead with my fingertips. Her hairdresser was fussing in the background, trying to get her to keep her head still.

"What I meant was, what you think about me picking you up?"

I knew that going to her house meant there was a likelihood that I was going to meet her parents. I didn't have a problem with that though. If they had raised Chelsea to be who she was, I figured it couldn't be that bad.

"Yeah, that's fine. I'll send you my location."

"Okay, see you soon."

* * *

Although it was located in Valsayn, Chelsea's home wasn't as grandiose as the one that I had manufactured for her in my mind. In fact, it was much smaller than the neighbours'. The split-level building was painted in a very light green. There was a large garden in the front, with flowers of all different shades and a host of potted plants. I rang the doorbell and stood waiting on the porch, twisting my watch around my wrist.

The giddy look on Chelsea's face when she greeted me was enough to ease any trepidation I had about standing at her doorstep. I couldn't exactly decipher what the hairdresser had done to her hair but it was straight like a pin today, a departure from the curls she usually wore. She wore a long maxi dress that skimmed her body and left so much to the imagination all at the same time. I made out some kind of gloss on her lips, which only made them look softer than they already were.

So damn pretty.

"Hurry up and come in so my mother would know you're real," she said. "I think she might still be recovering from the shock of when I told her that Carlisle didn't need to drop me to class today. That a boy wanted to do the honours."

I followed her into the home, my feet sinking into plush carpet. The spaces all flowed into one another, from the spotless kitchen to the regal dining room. There was an expensive looking grey couch in the living area, with real, live flowers sitting in a fancy vase on the glass-top table. Intricate African art flanked the dark walls and elaborate wooden figurines were positioned on freestanding shelves. In all, Chelsea's house looked like a carefully curated display, hardly befitting the playful, warm girl I'd been interacting with recently.

She stopped so suddenly that I crashed into her back and had to steady her. She turned around, looked me square in the eye and said abruptly, "This is the first time I've ever introduced my mother to a guy. I'm glad it's you."

"Wait, like you tryna make meh blush."

My insides clenched when I saw the duelling emotions on her face. The pleasure in her eyes, crossed with the way she was biting the corner of her lip. I swayed closer to her, needing to remind her that she wasn't alone in this. Until the recognition dawned. And then she turned and led me to the back of the house.

There was a garden there too, this one mostly with plants used for seasoning and small potted shrubs. Chelsea's mother was stooped down and had her back turned away from us, as she cut some pieces of aloes and arranged them in some sheets of newspaper lying next to her. When she turned to us and smiled at me, I just knew I'd seen her somewhere before.

Chelsea only vaguely favoured her mother. They had the

same round, dark honey-brown face and the same small, turned up button nose. But they didn't share any other facial features. Unlike Chelsea's large, expressive eyes, her mother's were small and shuttered.

"This is my mother, Lydia. Mummy this is Kyron. I have class with him at The Centre."

"Nice to meet you, Ms. Lydia," I said, shaking her hand. "And I'll drive safely, don't worry."

Her smile was guarded, brightened by just a measure of cordiality. She had the same assessing gaze that Carlisle had when I met him, but hers was even more scrutinizing.

"Hello, Kyron. I can't tell you the last time Chelsea introduced me to a boy, so that must say something about you," she said cursorily. Her eyes dissected me like she was attempting to see whatever it was that Chelsea saw. "And what's your last name, young man?"

Chelsea shifted with irritation beside me, but I didn't have any reservations in answering her mother's question.

"My full name is Kyron Grant."

"Oh. The Grants from Westmoorings. That is your family?"

"Mummy, he didn't come here to stand trial," Chelsea piped up from beside me. "Plus, at the rate you going, we gonna be late for class."

"Oh gosh, Chelsea, I can't ask a simple question?" Ms. Lydia posed, not looking the least bit remorseful.

"That is anything but a simple question, Mummy, and you know that."

My eyes shot back and forth between mother and daughter before I indulged the lady I hoped to impress.

"No, Ms. Lydia. I don't know any Grants from Westmoorings. My beginnings are a lot more humble than that, actually."

She disapproved – that much I knew. She was too refined to show it, but it was blatant in the way her lips pinched together before she showcased the most insincere of smiles. Chelsea was too smart to not sense the subtle shift in her mother's deportment. And at this point, I knew her well enough to tell that she was pissed off.

Just as Chelsea opened her mouth, I heard the voice of a man nearing, whom I imagined was Chelsea's father.

"Alright Lydia, I find the briefcase. I going back up the road."

It was only when Chelsea's father appeared at the glass sliding door, tall and broad-shouldered, with a high-priced suit jacket slung over his arm, that I realized where I had seen Ms. Lydia. It was in a video that I was watching when, ironically, I'd first met her daughter. And it was only then that I realized that I hadn't known Chelsea's surname.

"And this is my father, Peter Marchand," Chelsea said from beside me. "Though if you've been anywhere near a television recently, I sure an introduction not necessary."

No. There was absolutely no need, whatsoever, for an introduction.

* * *

CHELSEA

After maths class, Kyron offered to drop me off at Uncle Hinds' office. In the car, he was a bit quieter than his usual self and I missed the typical teasing we did with each other. It was crazy how I'd come to expect it from our interactions. As we neared the large glass building in the centre of town, I saw him fidget in his seat.

"So in two months, you could be the Prime Minister daughter," Kyron said from the driver's seat, his concentration staying on the road. It sounded more like he was speaking to himself than addressing me. He stared at that road like he was hell bent on keeping that promise he made to my mother about driving safely. Kyron was a straight shooter, so I was surprised that he hadn't come right out and made it clear that this was on his mind.

"Oh, so that's why you quiet so?" I asked.

Kyron didn't answer me, just made some kind of affirming murmur.

I shrugged. "Yup, that's what I meant when I was talking about a life that can be overwhelming at times."

Thick silence stretched and settled between us.

"I know you don't expect me to apologize for not telling you."

He finally shook his head, had this one-cheeked smile that bordered on cynical. "Nah. Trying to figure out how I didn't see it before now. You kinda fit the mould. No offense."

I shrugged. "None taken. I keep hoping that the less I talk about it, the more likely I'll wake up one day and go back to the life I used to have before this fiasco."

"You know that's not how it works, right?"

"A girl can dream," I told him.

"You don't like the fact that he in politics?"

"Is not just the politics."

When I glanced at Kyron again, his forehead was crinkled.

"Being a politician is a whole different beast from being Prime Minister. When you is Prime Minister, a whole country could blame you for everything that going wrong, you know? They could persecute you and ridicule you and keep your name in dey blasted mouth."

I struggled with my confession for unknown reasons, but Kyron had been forthcoming with me. So although I could only stand to look at his profile from the corner of my eye, I continued.

"Despite what he may do wrong in that role, he is someone's husband . . . someone's son . . . someone's father – my father!"

"I get that, Chels. That feeling like the public could forget that side of him and just nail him to the cross. But it's not really your job to protect him from that. And the country needs good leadership. From what I see of him, the man look like he would fit the bill."

And therein lay the dilemma. The voting public had no idea what they were getting themselves into, and that included Kyron. But I was loyal to my father. If he wanted to be Prime Minister, even with the rotting skeletons in his closet, it was my duty to want that for him too. I would wear a million ANP jerseys, and post twice as many statuses about how he would contribute to this nation, to see to it that his dream materialized.

"Yeah, you right. Is mostly me being selfish when I talk like that. He is a hard worker and a brilliant man. So yeah, not only *could* I be the Prime Minister's daughter in two months. I *should* be."

We pulled up in front the CCP's office and Kyron unlocked the door.

"So you think we could lime Saturday evening? Maybe go and eat somewhere nicer than the cafeteria in The Centre?" Kyron asked, with an overtone of casualness.

"You mean I ent scare you away yet?"

"Scared?" He steupsed. "You eh hear bout me or wah?"

I laughed loudly and accepted his invitation, warning him that it was conditioned on my parents giving it the 'okay'. When I hugged him, his chest felt hard against me. He had such an addictive guy scent about him too – clean and slightly citrusy. Saturday better and hurry up.

When I entered the office, I went in search of Uncle Hinds, only to find him rummaging through some paperwork at his desk, a strained expression on his face. This was only my second day at the internship. Even referring to it as such was bizarre, since I was here under pretext. I had to admit, though, that the first day had fascinated the nerdy side of me and I anticipated enjoying the experience for a few more weeks. When last I came, I was given a tour and shown how to work the phones. I was eager to start doing work that was more involved, though the atmosphere here seemed unhurried.

"Chelsea, just in time," he said, looking up.

"Afternoon, Uncle Hinds," I said, unable to bring myself

to address him with a formal title. "You want me to meet with Merlyn again today?" Merlyn was the militant office manager. She was an older woman who ran the office with an iron fist, but was so kind that it was easy to forget that despite what the lawyers thought, she was the one firmly in charge.

"Oh no. You'll be with one of the attorneys from here on out, Jennifer. I want to start you in intake. I think you could handle it."

He explained that intake was where the paperwork came in for all the crimes that were at the beginning stages of prosecution.

"So, you'll be labelling the folders and putting all the paperwork in them – police reports, interviews with witnesses, that kinda thing. And then Jennifer will show you how to organize them in the cabinets. She might ask you to do a memo on the progress of the cases too. Just depends."

"I didn't think it had any witnesses to crimes in this country," I told him.

Uncle Hinds gave a knowing laugh. "You mostly right. A lot of the interview sheets just have people saying they didn't see anything because they not trying to get killed. Jennifer went to catch the bank before it close so I'll show you where to set up."

I followed Uncle Hinds through the winding office until I eventually came to the small folding desk that he had set up for me, close to a door with Jennifer's nameplate plastered on it.

"I hope this okay," Uncle Hinds said apologetically, rubbing his head. "We short on space here. But at least here you away from most of the noise in the office."

"This is more than fine, Uncle Hinds. I actually didn't think

I'd even have a desk."

That admission seemed to put him more at ease and he pointed to a stack of documents on a separate table, split into different piles.

"Jennifer should be back soon, so for now you could go through the stuff that just came in this week. Each pile has all the documents we have so far on a specific case. Is not much but ..." he trailed off.

"Ok, I'll just look through the cabinet to see how the folders set up already and go from there. Merlyn showed me where the supplies and the copy machine are, so I should be fine."

I went to the table with the piles and noticed that atop each was a slip with the name of the crime written in dark marker ink. There were two robberies and a murder. Convinced that the murder would be the most interesting of the three, I grabbed that pile and settled in at my new workspace.

A few seconds later, I felt my heart galloping in my chest and my hand flew to my mouth. The victim in the murder case was an Anderson Brooks. It was clear to me that this was Kyron's Anderson because the details were the same. Same date. Chopped up body set on fire. Not surprisingly, there were no witness interviews in the pile. Mouths were typically sewn shut when it came to killings the likes of this one. This was the type of murder that was usually done to send a message. When my eyes landed on the pictures of his body parts, I tasted bile in my throat.

"Good Lord," I whispered to myself.

When I got close to the bottom of the pile, shock bolted through my body. There was a page titled, 'SUSPECTS', but there was only one name written. Instantly, I recalled Kyron's doubt that anyone was even going to be held responsible for killing his friend. Quite frankly, I'd shared that scepticism. I grabbed my phone from my bag to text Kyron. He wasn't going to believe that an investigative team had already submitted a file on Anderson, identifying some man named Grafton Walters as the one who'd orchestrated the murder.

Chapter 8

KYRON

At the entrance of the mill stood a guy I didn't recognize. He was an Indian fella with hair neatly slicked back away from his forehead. He was likely just a few years older than I was, and looked apprehensive about the implications of my being there.

"Who you is, youth man? What you doing here?" he demanded. He wore a dark blue uniform, topped by a cap that hid most of his eyes. I couldn't continue to look at him without thinking about Anderson, when he was young and eager to prove himself. I wondered if he was unsuspecting as Anderson had been or if he knew what this work entailed and considered the risk worth it.

"I here to see Grafton Walters," I replied, with more tremors in my voice than I was willing to concede.

On a harsh and derisive laugh, he reached to the waist of his pants for something that was wedged there.

"I eh think I hear you properly. Say that again? Who it is you say you come here to see?" he asked, his stance rigid.

Gary's voice interrupted. "Ease up dey, Avinash. Dat is the boss man son."

I released the breath that I hadn't realized I was holding. Gary crooked his finger at me, and my steps fell beside his as we walked to the back. Without the sounds of the heavy machinery, the floor of the mill was eerily quiet, with only a tangible and ominous hollowness in the air. My legs felt like concrete had been poured into them, and I wasn't sure how I managed to put one in front the other and line them up to head in the direction of my father's office.

"Young Walters, you hadda watch yourself when you coming up here," Gary said.

I couldn't respond. I was concentrating on this sinister atmosphere that only lent more credence to what Chelsea had texted me two days before. How had I not noticed it the last time I was here?

"You hear meh?" he asked.

"Yeah, yeah," I said absentmindedly.

When I crossed the doorway, I saw my father flipping through some papers, a taut expression on his face.

"Boss," Gary called out to him.

When my father looked up, his eyes grew tight with apparent worry, in a way that belied his customary stoicism.

"What you doing here, Kyron!" he declared, rather than

asked.

Gary looked uncomfortable. "I had to bring him inside, Boss. Is only Avinash covering the front and –"

My father cut him off with a commanding slant of his head, signalling for him to leave. This was an imperious side of him that I had never been privy to, and which rattled me. The side I only knew about theoretically, having never seen it in action. Gary's absence left me exposed, to confront the question of whether I had the gumption to follow through with my intent when I had headed here.

After an extended, charged pause, I asked, "So that's the most you think of my mother? That she only good enough to be with a murderer?" My voice was calm and steadier than I had anticipated.

"Have a seat, Kyron," he ordered.

With only slight hesitation, I obeyed.

"Now, I not going to speculate as to where you getting your news from –"

"Doh take me for no fool," I interrupted, swallowing my nervousness. "You feel is now I know you sellin' coke? Twelve years. That is how old I was." I scoffed at the memory. "Anderson had come to pick meh up from coaching school. Bawl how he had one more run to make for you. Didn't want Ma to worry by leaving me waiting on the field for too long so he decided to just take me along for the ride."

The only signs that he was even listening to me were his mirthless smirk and the slight flaring of his nostrils.

"I had always wondered how come you had so much money. I used to think, 'maybe my father is a doctor in secret. Or a banker.' And then when I found out what was really going on ..." I couldn't finish my sentence.

"Kyron, I know you don't honestly think your father in the business of killing anybody. And Anderson? The young man whom I brought so close to my own family? Whose mother's house I just stood in as she mourned?"

I bristled at the use of the word *family* to describe whatever sham of an arrangement we had going on. But the discomfort was soon overshadowed by confusion.

"To tell you the truth, I doh know what to think. I doh even know who you is," I said, lifting my hands in the air and letting them fall on my lap.

"Well, you obviously know me well enough to come grand charging here nine o'clock on a Friday night, flinging accusations all over the place," he said.

"So you could watch me in my eye and tell me you didn't do that." My voice sounded strange, tortured, even to my own ears. "That you didn't hack up a woman son and then pay to put him in the ground."

He tented his fingers in front his face before addressing me. His eyes were steel itself.

"Kyron, I really don't care who you been talking to. You mustn't believe everything you hear, son," he commanded smoothly. I felt gullible, nauseated by the thought that this was how he got people to idolize him and do his bidding. By speaking with conviction, as if his words were gospel by virtue of his saying them.

"Yeah, I do plenty in my day," he continued. "More bad than good since you wanna talk man to man. But I would never intentionally hurt you. The same goes for your mother. And I refuse to say another word on this ridiculous matter."

I had no concrete basis to doubt what he was saying, and yet, I had every reason in the world to distrust him. I only knew what he showed himself to be, which was a generous, if aloof man. If he was telling the truth about not being involved, then he was the same indifferent man I'd always known him to be. If he was lying, and he really was some kind of covert killer, then that meant that he had kept his ugly world separate from my mother and me, so there would be no stigma attached to our name. How was it possible to be so sickened by someone and grateful to him in the same moment? I was ready to bolt through the door but wanted to stay rooted to where I sat until he dispelled my suspicions. If only he could just convince me of the kind of person he truly was.

My father spoke with a firm voice, his shoulders hunched, which somehow made him seem bigger, impregnable.

"Look here, Kyron. What I do and ent do in my life is none of your concern ... dat have no effect on you. You have your own life to live." With a nonchalant shrug, he began shuffling some papers on his desk. He dismissed me with that same distant expression he wore at Anderson's wake. My eyes didn't meet his half-lidded gaze again. Instead, I rose from the chair and inched away from his office, even more tormented than when I had arrived.

* * *

"Or else I won't do the address in Tobago."

Even my toes trembled, but I didn't retract the words that hung in the air. The clacking of his fingertips against the keyboard ceased. Daddy reclined in his chair and strummed his fingers on his stomach, looking like a czar assessing the audacity of an out-of-line subject. A trace of derision shone in his dark eyes and a taut rope of understanding stretched between us as we regarded each other, neither of us willing to look away.

He wasn't doing well in Tobago, particularly with younger voters. And they made up a large chunk of the electorate. When questioned by news reporters in the streets, their responses had been unanimous, just variations of the same sentiment.

"Something about that man," they said, usually with a slight shake of the head. They couldn't quite trust what they attempted to put into words. But I knew what they alluded to; I saw my father put it on each day when he left the house. A slickness, almost. He needed both the Tobago East and West seats to have a legitimate chance of winning the election. And I, his unwilling orator, was his bridge to them. I'd given a salutatory at my form five graduation that had my class in tears. He knew that I could take the stage and perform, formulate an address with all the right words. One that would grab them by the throat. He understood that I would resonate with them in a way he never could. Even though my love of words was normally problematic for him, he had his convenient uses for it.

"What you just say?" he pressed. His question, albeit voiced quietly, pierced the room.

I was wading in unchartered waters. I weaselled around

situations. I didn't put ultimatums to my father. And I'd certainly never attempted to bargain with something so important to him, so critical to his future.

"I won't do the Tobago address if you don't allow me to go. Not when I hardly ask for anything in the first place."

He clenched his jaw and his eyes shrunk as they assessed me, tested my seriousness. I kept my head level, my eyes peeled on his. Even as I swallowed over the wad of nervousness in my throat, I tried to make that movement as inconspicuous as possible. He was ticked, that much I knew. But I didn't miss the begrudging respect there either. Just as I began wondering which would win out, he broke eye contact and directed his attention to his laptop again. At his silent consent, a smirk tugged at my lips.

* * *

If this were any other guy, I would have felt an immense amount of trepidation at being so far into San Fernando and still uninformed as to our destination.

After SAT class today, Kyron had refused to divulge any information regarding our date, only telling me to wear something comfortable. And so Dahlia had called to video chat around two o'clock, overexcited and finicky, to help with choosing an outfit for this, my first date. She started off by vetoing three dresses. Then she suggested a romper because she had read some online magazine that said Capricorns should show their playful side this month, but she changed her mind, mumbling something about the moon. Had I put up with her indecision for much longer, I would be sitting in Kyron's car wearing drawers and a pair of rubber slippers. So I settled on an off-shoulder cream top, white jeans and brown sandals, only succumbing to her insistence that I wear my hair loose and curly.

"I wonder if I can bribe you," I pondered aloud. "Ah sure I have something in my bag that I can seduce you with in exchange for a clue, at least."

"You trust me?" he asked without looking at me, his right hand firmly on the steering wheel, his left on the stick.

"I suppose I do. As much as I can trust someone I've only known for a few weeks." Even I could admit it felt longer than that.

"I'll take that. And the answer to your question is 'no'. I'm not bribable, as a general principle. And doh be watching meh with dem puppy-dog eyes either. Stop dat."

I laughed at his perception and relaxed in the passenger seat. We fell into that contented silence thing that we'd been doing lately when we found ourselves alone. Kyron drove fast without being reckless. He hardly took his eyes off the road, as I had realized was his pattern. He'd complied with his own directive to me to dress casually, wearing a plain black v-neck jersey, dark jeans, and a black cap that wasn't pulled all the way down on his head. I was happy the hat left his eyes exposed. While I had never understood when girls fawned over a guy's eyes, Kyron had the most beautiful eyes I'd ever seen. His were dark and deep, and he used them like he knew their power. As if to prove my point, his gaze slid over to me.

"You look nice, Chels."

"Thanks. I wasn't too sure what to wear. You didn't give me much help in that area."

He paused before responding. "Didn't matter what you wore, exactly. I was just hoping you wouldn't back out."

There was an unmistakable vulnerability in his tone, so I didn't bother telling him what I had to barter to be with him right now.

"So I think we can safely say that your parents don't like me."

"Well, the fact that I'm sitting in this car is a testament to their not hating you," I responded, looking at his profile.

"That's comforting," he said, grinning. "Your father's intense."

"My father's insane," I said, coaxing a full laugh out of him.

"I get it though. I'm not exactly unaccustomed to that type of strong personality. That's why I picked here for our date." It was only when I tore my eyes from him that I realized we were pulling into a parking lot in La Romain.

He hurried to explain. "I figure with all you have going on ... election ... SATs ... we could just come here and forget about all that for a while. Just chill."

There was no disguising my look of incredulity and I'm sure that Kyron saw the way I lit up. And then he looked reassured about his decision on selecting a game room for a first date. I had seen this place advertised regularly on television and wasn't the slightest bit ashamed that I had wanted to visit. They boasted miniature bowling, bumper cars, ice ball and a host of arcade games that would make children, and big horses like me, giddy.

I couldn't remember the last time I had just ... played.

"So here good?" Kyron asked.

"Good?" I asked, staring through the windshield. "I studying if I walk with enough cash to get all the tokens I might need. I not sure you understand the damage I could do inside this place."

"A girl after my own heart. Just for that, you could have all the tokens you want."

I feigned surprise, grasping my chest. "Aye aye, you livin' large!"

Kyron stroked his chin. "Well, you know your boy is a big spender."

I shoved him playfully and we headed inside. Kyron bought enough tokens to fill both front pockets, so we wouldn't have to keep returning to the front when we ran out. We started at the bumper cars and moved our way around the room. We lingered at each game, sometimes doing two rounds, caught up in the excitement of the competition. By the time we got to mini basketball he had me doubling over in laughter with his antics. He riled up an imaginary crowd by waving his hands, and turned his cap so that the brim was at the back of his head. Blocking and dodging the imaginary fellas on the other team, he stuck his tongue out like Michael Jordan and made a big to-do when he made the basket. I extended my pretend pompoms in the air and plastered a perky smile on my face. The fact that the basketball area couldn't be more than four square feet only added to the absurdity of our conduct.

When I saw him readying to make another play, I joined in, though I didn't know a thing about basketball. I shuffled to the left and shimmied to the right, mimicking players I had seen on television, in hopes that I could stop his charging towards the rim. I was certain that I looked like a fool but Kyron made a great show of not being able to get by me. My chest fell against his forearm that held the basketball and his smell washed over me like it did the day he asked me out. I held my hands up to further prevent him from going past me but that just made my body angle towards him even more. His face was centimetres away from mine and he couldn't stop staring, his teeth tugging at his bottom lip.

"So this is how you plan to distract meh? By flirting?" he asked softly.

"I don't flirt," I answered, borrowing his words.

He turned to the side, his left shoulder pressed against me, and began bouncing the ball up and down.

"And after all this, I still gonna make the basket," he said.

"With that weak jump shot ah yours? Yeah, sure." I knew I would pay for throwing talk at him.

"And what I gonna get when I do? How exactly you plan on congratulating me?"

In a brief moment of insanity, with an incoherent thought rushing from my mouth before I could even retract it, I answered him. "A kiss."

The ball stopped bouncing and the corner of his eyes darted directly to me. His lips parted in a way that made me want to simultaneously take back what I'd just said and repeat it. And then, with a swift turn, he pivoted away from me, curled his elbows, and scored what I imagined would have been a three-point shot on an ordinary basketball court.

He sidled up close to me and leaned close to my ear. "Don't

worry, I won't make you pay up now." His hand fell on the curve in my back, above the waist of my jeans, making my breathing difficult. Kyron steered me to the miniature bowling area and put in some tokens to start a new game. I was grateful when we broke contact because my nerve endings were all helter-skelter. I didn't understand how he could have that effect on me with just a touch. And what was it about his voice that left my brain so scattered?

"So since your basketball game could use some improvement, maybe you'll fare a little better at bowling," he said.

I couldn't bowl to save my life. When I went on vacation in the States to visit my mother's side of the family, we would always go to some bowling alleys. But I would either release the ball too early or take horrible aim.

"I am a master bowler," I said. "So prepare to be impressed."

"Alright, I see you Chels. I hope you is not all talk, you know."

My eyes were slanted at him, challenging. Kyron started the game and stood to the side so that I could take my turn. He crossed his arms over his chest, looking entertained. I reached for the ball and shimmied my fingers into the holes. I lined myself up against the alley and inched the tips of my shoes as close to the line as they could go without it being considered cheating.

"Toes kinda close there."

"Stop tryna put your jumbie on me, please," I said, concentrating. With the ball at eye-level, I envisioned where I wanted it to land and leaned over so that I was angled against the alley just right. Confident that this position would allow me to knock down at least half of the pins, I released the ball with just enough force. About one second into its journey, it hung to the far left and went straight into the gutter.

Kyron winced.

"Well, you definitely have a strong throw," he said. "Would you mind if I gave a few pointers?"

"Point away," I said. "Clearly, I need it."

"Okay, so you might wanna start by picturing a line in your mind. Just imagine a line running from your toes to the pins and send the ball straight down that pretend line. Try not to put too much strength in it though. That will just pull your swing off the line." He stood at my side, going through the motions as if he were throwing an actual ball down the alley.

I did as Kyron instructed, envisioning the line.

"Okay, now just take a deep breath – that'll help you stay relaxed."

Again, I did as he coached. Breath. Line. Less strength. And then ... gutter. My determination flared. I didn't want to ask him to explain again but I didn't want a stupid ball to get the better of me either.

"So you gonna stand up there and continue to pretend bowl or you gonna come and help me?"

After a moment's pause, he waltzed up behind me and curved his arms around mine.

"Okay, if you want to make your swing relaxed, you have to start in the stance. Bring the ball to waist level like this," he directed, easing my orange bowling ball down until it was at my waist.

"Chels, you have to relax your hands, sweetheart. You have

the thing in a death grip."

With him behind me, his warm chest pressed against my back, I wasn't even sure I could spell the word 'relax'.

"Okay, try this. Since you're holding the ball with your right hand, move your right foot back so you could balance better." He gave me a moment to reposition my legs.

"Good. Okay, now squeeze the ball as hard as you can for like ten seconds."

I heeded his advice, tensing my fingers on the ball.

"Ok, ease up on your grip now. Feel the difference?"

I nodded, my hair brushing up against his neck.

"Now what?"

"Now, answer your phone," Kyron said, releasing me suddenly.

It was only when our bodies separated that I realized that my back pocket was vibrating. I sent the ball down the alley and reached for my phone, only to hear Shelly-Ann on the other line.

"Your grandmother want to talk to you."

"Now, Shelly-Ann? I kinda in the middle of something."

"Like what? A hot date?" she asked, laughing. "Girl, if she didn't wanna talk to you now, you think I would be callin' you now?" she asked with a bite to her voice.

"Okay, put her on the phone."

I covered the phone and mouthed my apologies to Kyron, who'd put a few feet of distance between us and was standing with his hands clasped behind his neck. Looking unbothered at the intrusion, he motioned his head to let me know that he was going to find us a table at the food court.

Gramma came on the phone and I heard her clearing her

throat.

"Chelsea, darlin'." Her voice was no weaker than when last I heard it so it didn't seem as if something was wrong.

"Yes, Gramma, I here. What going on?"

"So something have to be goin' on for meh to want to hear meh grandchile voice? But I never see more."

"No, no Gramma, that's not what I mean." The idea that my first date was being interrupted with casual conversation with my grandmother, of all people, could only be expected from my life.

"How you feeling, Gramma?" I asked, heading off in search of Kyron.

"What to tell you, meh chile? All about huttin' meh, pain everywhere. Meh head. Meh eye. Meh leg dem feel like dey want to fall off. But I good still, you know."

"You sure you good with all dem ting going on?"

"Yes, yes. But hear what I really call to tell you eh. Is about what I dream last night. And ah want you to listen good."

I felt my skin prickle and the hairs on my skin stand on end. I took a seat opposite Kyron, who'd found us a clean table at the far end of the food court, away from a lot of the noise. When he looked at me enquiringly, I lifted my shoulders to let him know that I didn't know the direction of this conversation either.

"What kinda dream is that?"

"Well girl, we was on this big boat, me and you. We was travelling whole night. And it finally reach the shore. Next ting you know, you bawl, 'Gramma, I coming off right here'."

I sat transfixed, attempting to decode what she was telling me.

"Well girl, when ah tell you I get a shock when you say that. But I didn't try to stop you. No sah!"

She inhaled deeply and continued.

"You ask the captain to let you off one time. And then you went and stand up on the shore. If you see how you stand up straight, straight. You had a briefcase in your hand too. And you was wearing a pretty, pretty long dress, flowing on the ground."

If only she could see the folds in my forehead, which spoke of my bewilderment as to the meaning of the dream.

"What happened after that?"

"Well the boat was getting ready to leave, eh. And I just stand up on the deck, watching you on the shore. And then it look like you couldn't decide what to do."

I didn't understand the tension bubbling in me.

"The captain pull up the anchor. Horn start to blow. And then you call out to meh loud. Ask meh if you should go. All that time the captain done start the engine, you know. The boat was done rumbling already."

"And what you said, Gramma?"

"Well girl, I couldn't talk. You hear meh? I couldn't find meh voice, ah tellin' you. But before I coulda even find the words, you say, 'Gramma, I goin'. Meh briefcase done pack already.' And you walk off. Well girl, I wake up schupid after that."

My grandmother had told me about her *visitations from heaven* before. But she had never dreamed me. Moreover, I didn't know the dream protocol. Was I supposed to know what all of this meant? Was I supposed to wait for her to decrypt it for me?

"So what all that mean Gramma?"

"Well dat is not for me to know, meh chile. That dream come for you. But I believe you will find out in due time. Just know Gramma love you. Alright?"

"Alright, Gramma. Love you too."

"You have to go?" Kyron asked when I ended the call.

"No, no. Just my grandmother telling me about a dream she had."

He nodded. "Everything okay?"

"I hope so." I smiled, hoping to bring back the lightness we had before the phone call, but my grandmother's words lingered.

During our conversation, there'd been a sureness in her tone. The kind that my father tried to manufacture when he promised his supporters a better tomorrow. She'd even sounded more convicted than Dahlia sermonizing about ruling planets and rising signs. What Gramma saw in her sleep was bound to happen. It always did. If only I knew what it was.

Chapter 9

KYRON

It was just before midnight and the party was picking up some steam. The music was loud, the beats reverberating within my chest and energizing me. We were at a club in Bon Accord, a cool space with an oversized thatched roof and trees dotting the compound. The DJ began playing a Machel tune and a host of sideline-posers rushed to the dance floor, gaining confidence to move in on the ladies they'd been eyeing. The breeze carried with it a light chill, cooling the sweaty dancers on the middle of the floor. Red and blue strobe lights darted wildly from the ceiling. I pitied the girl Dinel was dancing with. Every time she tried to pull away, he drew her back at the waist for another relentless wine. Andrew and I were on the right hand side of the club, both of us drinking a Carib. Shawn, my cousin from Mason Hall who'd brought us here, was chatting up the female bartender.

We were in Tobago for a football match against Signal Hill, the perennial Intercol champs. Dem fellas, though still in their teens, were built like strapping, grown men. Forests of chest hair, long, wiry beards and muscles bulging all over the place. We hadn't had delusions about winning, and were only glad for the opportunity. But we took the match – five goals to four – with a nerve-wracking finish that had almost sent Coach Joseph to the emergency room. He couldn't catch himself after the win and told us he didn't care what the hell we did for the rest of the weekend, as long as we were back at the guesthouse before three o'clock tomorrow so that we could catch the boat back to Trinidad. So Shawn picked up Andrew, Dinel and me, assuring us that the vibes here was nice.

"So what going on with you and Chelsea?" Andrew asked out of nowhere, as he peered at a pretty, short girl wearing a white mini skirt.

"What you mean?"

He refocused on me and explained, "Dinel tell meh she pass by the field the other night. And well, he say you was movin' like da is your gyul."

I hadn't spoken to Andrew about Chelsea. In fact, other than my mother that night in the car, I hadn't spoken to anyone about her. Granted, the fellas knew about Daneen almost as soon as we started limin', mostly because she'd made no secret of it. But getting to know Chelsea was like unwrapping a present slowly. I wanted to savour the experience for myself. I didn't care for random fellas knowing about how I felt when I was around her.

Or how crazy soft her skin was. Or how running around playing games with her last week, acting like some little children, was the most fun I'd had with any girl, ever.

"You asking for you, or you asking to carry news?"

Andrew looked offended but that was of no concern to me. He damn well knew his mouth couldn't hold water.

"You cut meh with dat one, General Grant. You cut meh deep."

"Eh nothing to talk about in any event. We cool, you know?" Whatever was going on between Chelsea and me was our business. The last thing I wanted was her name in people's mouths, especially given who her father was.

"So ... nothing going on?"

It was more like whatever was going on likely didn't stand a chance of lasting, especially given the information she'd passed on to me regarding my father's involvement with Anderson's death. Hell, it wasn't realistic to even want a relationship with her. So I knew the reason I was so tight-lipped about my time with her was because I understood how fleeting it was, and I had no idea of how long I had left. I had every right to be protective.

"Let meh rephrase the question, cause you acting like ah talking a different language," Andrew said. "If I ask her to go out, it goh be a scene?"

My eyes flew over to him, annoyed. I remembered that time we were in that first SAT class together, and I saw Andrew wink at Chelsea. I hadn't thought anything of it since that day because Chelsea had never seemed interested. Knowing her as I did now, it was clear that she didn't want him like that. But the fact that he seemed genuinely interested in her messed with my head.

My response was stiff. "Chelsea off-limits, Andrew."

"Buy you just say – "

"I know you hear what the hell I just say. We cool and all but you doh wanna push meh on this one."

"Alright boss," he said, holding up his hands in mock surrender. "I eh trying to mess up your situation. And you is meh boy and everything. But if ah ketch you slippin' I movin' in on your gyul eh. Ah tellin' you dat from now."

He shrugged, and I wanted to cuff the smug look off of his damn face. He moved away to dance on the girl he was ogling earlier. A triumphant smile decorated her lips as she pushed back on him and looked over her shoulder to confirm the identity of the person that had taken up residence there. I wasn't a big party fella but I didn't go to a party to hold up the wall either. So by now, I would usually be dancing with a good-looking girl too. But I had come in here thinking about Chelsea and the conversation with Andrew only set me on edge even further.

While we'd texted and spoken on the phone during the week, it was mostly about class stuff. She'd told me she was trying to get into this prestigious writing program at Georgetown and really needed to ace the verbal. And I was mindful of what the Howard coaches had said about not losing focus on getting good scores. So when we'd spoken, it was mostly to work through a lot of questions together, and she had been busy with ANP stuff for much of the week. In the middle of all of that, she'd admitted she had a good time on the date. But I knew that didn't necessarily mean that she wanted to be with me. And then there was the issue of that bombshell she'd dropped regarding my father. I couldn't exactly continue to feign ignorance about his identity for much longer, but I was tight as hell, knowing that Chelsea would likely call things off with us when I eventually told her.

She'd told me that she and her parents would be in Tobago this weekend, as they had a Public Meeting in Shaw Park. Her father wanted her to deliver an address but she'd been stalling on whether or not she would accept. It was after twelve now and she was probably still at the meeting. The fellas each had a girl positioned against them and they were in their glee. Pointing their bottlenecks in the air, they signalled their bliss at being young, drunk and the new holders of bragging rights after our victory against Signal Hill. And there I was, grabbing my phone from my back pocket and opening up the most recent dialogue box to text the girl I just couldn't get off my mind.

ME: Can I see you tonight?

* * *

CHELSEA

I sat with my legs crossed neatly at the ankles, my leather folder perched in my lap, and I listened to my father introduce me to the crowd, the pride in his voice almost tangible.

"You've heard me reference her many times on the

campaign trail," he began, with measured pontification. "And I know when you hear her speak with such certainty ... with such insight ... with wisdom that belies her tender age ... that you will see her as I do. That this young lady will be at the forefront of Trinidad and Tobago politics in the years to come."

When I presented my address to my father, he was convinced that it would cement his place in the election race. Having the electorate hear the impassioned and articulate call to arms from his mere seventeen-year-old daughter was political gold. But even as I practiced in front the mirror, got into character and finessed my cadence and pauses, I promised myself that this was the last time. I would do my father's bidding this one last time. Then I would no longer be used as a pawn. As for tonight though, I'd give them the best show they'd ever seen, issuing the clarion call on behalf of this bloody impostor.

"As the Good Book says, 'out of the mouth of babes and sucklings'. So please help me welcome my daughter, my pride and joy, and a concerned citizen of this blessed twin-island republic, Ms. Chelsea Marchand."

Dressed like British royalty in a collarless navy-blue skirt suit, I approached the podium, confidence in my stride. My attire had been meticulously assembled – a jacket cinched in at the waist and flared over the hips, an exquisitely tailored skirt just skimming the top of my calves and shiny patent leather heels. Hair pulled back in a low, sleek bun to emphasize maturity and sophistication. I could practically feel their regard for my commanding appearance.

And then, with a strong, even voice, I told them. I told them that their united sojourn to Shaw Park, thousands strong, was indicative of the monumental nature of this election. I said from Bethel to Belle Garden, Plymouth to Pembroke, all Tobagonians could demand and expect accountability from Dr. Peter Marchand.

And at the same time, I swallowed the bitterness in my mouth, remembering that he wouldn't know what accountability meant if it slapped him in the face. That for years, he took payoffs for doing audits for big companies trying to hide dirty money.

Feeding off the energy of the crowd, I manipulated my tempo and adjusted my volume to deliver a compelling message. I clenched my fists when I wished to appear authoritative and pointed a delicate finger when I sought to evoke trust. I promised them that they could comb through the entire nation, search every nook, cranny and crevice, and wouldn't find a better role model for their children.

And deep in my belly still sat the horror and dread I felt years ago, when he assured Mummy and me that we didn't have to worry about him ending up like Mr. Lezama.

I urged the ANP supporters to rally every nephew, every niece, and every nennen. To pack up their vans and their maxis, and go dip their finger against tyranny … dip their finger against anarchy … and dip their finger for democracy.

And I remembered my tipping point, a week and a half ago. When I'd brought my father the name of a "big-fish" from the second day of my internship, he'd seemed only marginally satisfied. Then, he said Grafton Walters was … an acquaintance, and he wasn't yet prepared to use him as the sacrificial lamb. But he expressed his confidence in me, that I could dig around further and get him what he needed.

My mother approached the podium and mopped my damp brow with a soft, embroidered handkerchief, one of Christopher's suggestions when we'd done a run-through of my address. The crowd roared their approval, the music an accompaniment to their raucous endorsement. I bid them goodnight, gathered my folder and kissed my parents on their cheeks, in turn. I took my seat, my shoulders thrown back, my chin high. Only then did I allow myself to really feel the disgust coursing through me. When I reached for my phone to text Kyron about speaking to him before I went to bed, I saw that he'd already beaten me to it.

* * *

My parents had a four-bedroom house in Signal Hill, which was more like a cozy, modern cottage. They'd purchased it from an older man who was eager to sell and move to Trinidad with his family. It took them a year to gut and restore it from top to bottom but they retained most of the dark wood, which now had just the right amount of shine because of its age. The miniature palm trees in the yard were also a fortunate inheritance from the previous owner. To the side of the house were a patio and a medium-sized pool, adorned with rustic brickwork on its edge. Lounge chairs and a large umbrella made the space look every inch the oasis my mother had envisioned and demanded of her landscaper. Because the house wasn't built with concrete, it was usually cool, and tonight was no exception.

Since it was too late to go out, I'd responded to Kyron asking him if he'd be fine with coming by the house. My father had been so pleased with my performance that my reward was his allowing me to spend some time with him. My mother, however, had begged my assurance that this 'thing' was just a fleeting 'teenagers having fun' kind of situation. When I'd refused to answer her, she'd turned on her heel and retreated to her room without another word.

I bathed and changed into a new pajama set, which was really some purple cotton shorts and a matching t-shirt. As soon as I pulled my hair into a loose ponytail, the phone vibrated on the bed, letting me know that Kyron was here. I ran downstairs, bare feet padding against the tile, and opened the gate for him to park in the garage.

"Whose car?" I asked through the window as he reversed into the spot.

"Cousin own. He busy chatting up this girl in the club so he just give meh the keys."

As soon as he got out of the car, Kyron pulled me into his arms, in a hug that was strong and sure. His hands were looped around my waist and I tiptoed to lean into him as much as my body allowed. I snickered a bit at our juxtapositions. He smelled like expensive cologne and I smelled like soap. My outfit was fitting for bed and he was dressed for a party. And yet, I couldn't think of anywhere I would have rather been.

He released me and touched my nose on the same spot that my finger often landed when I was being contemplative.

"Hey, pretty girl," he said softly.

"Hey, you," I said, not understanding my sudden shyness.

I took his hand and led him to the lounge chairs furthest away from the house, flipping the light switch on the way. The area was bathed in just enough of a glow to allow us to see each other clearly.

"You want something to drink?" I asked.

He shook his head and I settled into my chair, curling my right leg underneath me as I often did. We sat facing each other, with just a foot of space between us. He wore grey jeans, a white Lacoste jersey, and a silver watch I'd never seen on him before. Absorbing how handsome he was made my nerve endings tingle, and I tried not to think about the girls who'd be coming on to him tonight. That spike of jealousy was so foreign that it took a second to register what it was.

"How it went?" he asked, leaning into me slightly. "Chelsea for Prime Minister 2035?"

As I'd only mentioned the address to Kyron in passing, I'd forgotten I'd told him about it.

"Hardly," I said, rolling my eyes. "I gave them what they asked for though. So I'm done with their little games."

"Games? You think this was a set up?" Kyron asked.

"I know it was. My father feel he slick. There's this powerful feeling you get when you in control of a crowd like that. When they waiting to hear what you gonna say next. When you can pull them in with your words. He passed that trait down to me. That feeling is like a drug though. And he wants me to start to get high on it." I didn't plan on indicting my father in front of Kyron, and a part of me felt disloyal even speaking as much as I did. But another part of me was appreciative for the catharsis.

"Sounds like you resisting."

"I think a part of me fears that what he does with those people is the same thing he does with me. Controls just because he can."

"I doubt that for some reason. The need for control usually has a backstory," Kyron said, bringing his chair closer to mine, so that our knees practically skimmed each other.

"Hmph, if you knew him like I did, you wouldn't give him so much credit."

"So this was really it? Your last act of compliance? You is a rebel now?" The look in his eyes was an enthralling mix of humour and curiosity.

"Fight the power!" I declared half-heartedly, holding up a wavering right fist.

He chuckled, making my insides twist and bunch up.

"What it is you want, Chels? I mean, what is it that you get up wanting?"

"That's the ultimate paradox, you know? It so illogical to want to trust that your parents know what's best for you, and at the same time, trust that you, with your naïve seventeen-year-old self, can possibly know better."

"There's a fine line between crossing over from the former into the latter," Kyron said pensively.

"Tell me when it happens, then," I said, pushing against his knee. "Do I cross it on the morning of my eighteenth birthday? I'll wake up and feel it in meh bones?" I was looking to Kyron like he really had the answers.

Kyron shrugged. "I'll let you know when I find out."

"But you don't have that issue though. From what you've told me, your mother just wants you to 'do you'. And your father ... well, I know he not dictating your pace like that."

"True. But sometimes you could be trying to escape what's in your own mind. The things you tell your own self. I went to see my father last week Friday," Kyron added. His confession surprised me because I was cognizant of how little he had to do with his father. I wondered about the motivation for the visit but could easily discern from his expression that it hadn't been a pleasant encounter.

"What did you all quarrel about?"

A dark look crested his face before he answered. "A few different things actually. But it was a realization moment for me too."

"How so?"

"I dunno. I guess, despite the fact that he was never really there for us in the physical sense, I still wanted to hear him just come out and say I could go ahead and live my own life, you know? Come from behind his shadow. Weird right?"

"Doesn't sound weird to me," I explained. "When push come to shove, they're still your parents. I don't know about my parents though. I feel like I might be waiting from now till eternity trying to please them."

Kyron nodded his understanding. "Yeah. Even the longest rope has an end though," he said. And then a silence settled in the little space that remained between our bodies, filled with unspoken thoughts.

"Andrew asked me about us," Kyron said softly.

"Asked what about us?"

"If he'd be intruding on anything if he asked you to go out." Kyron searched my eyes for an answer that I wouldn't give. What did he expect me to say? Was there anything to intrude on? There wasn't even an 'us'.

I found myself licking my lips, seeking a diversion from

having to respond to the question.

"That's why you sitting here? Watching me like that? Because of Andrew?"

He looked more intrigued than affronted. "Nope. I came to collect on your debt."

"Huh?"

Kyron leaned into me and dipped his mouth close to mine, leaving a mere inch between our lips. My breath stalled. If all of my emotions showed on my face, like he'd said, then all of his showed in his eyes. They were even darker and deeper than usual, which only seemed to highlight the confidence and uncertainty I saw in them.

"Remember how you said you were gonna congratulate me on my weak jump shot?"

He moved in even closer and both of us were practically rocking with anticipation now. The sounds around us intensified. The breeze. The car passing down the gravelly street. He placed his right hand around the back of my neck, just under my ponytail, and pulled me in gently. I couldn't stop the shivers rippling through me. But Kyron didn't bridge that final gap between us. Like that first time he'd texted me, allowing me to have the final say. Some unnamed emotion lodged in my throat and that only made my skin flush even more. Our eagerness matched each other's but yet, he remained frozen, waiting for me.

"Congratulations," I breathed, sealing his lips with mine.

Chapter 10

CHELSEA

Jennifer plopped a dusty, brown box on my desk, making me jump in my seat. Now that I was a few weeks into my internship and she had realized how much work I could take on, she didn't hesitate to assign me some of the heavier cases. I hoped she wasn't getting too comfortable though, as the new school term was about to start next week and any extra time I had would be consumed by my final SAT prep.

"Okay, Chelsea. I know you working on the Hosein case but we have some more on Anderson Brooks. So, you know ..." She didn't explain any further, just opted to make some kind of motioning with her hands signalling, presumably, that I needed to work on getting the new documents in the case file.

"No problem, Jennifer. I'll get to that now."

I sorted through the new material the investigators had submitted. Unsurprisingly, there still weren't any witnesses to the crime and there wasn't a stitch of DNA evidence to speak of.

"Is a wonder anything does get prosecuted in this place," I murmured under my breath, as I lugged the box over to the copy machine.

As I prepared to make the copies, I sorted through some of the new information they'd gathered. There was an interview with Anderson's mother and I skimmed it before I ran it through the machine. There wasn't any picture of her but I could practically feel her pain in the words the investigator had transcribed. I couldn't escape the thought that Anderson was dead at twenty-five, all his aspirations buried with him. Did he have moments like mine, when he dithered about the direction of his life? If he had known his fate, how different would his life choices have been? I shook off the thoughts. I didn't have the luxury of extensive theorizing. I grabbed the next set of papers and began working through them. The 'SUSPECTS' sheet was still the same, with that single name, Grafton Walters. My blood crawled with the memory of my father alluding to having some affiliation with him. I dared not even think about the ways that he could be associated with a suspected murderer.

And then my eye caught another document in the stack that hadn't been there before. It was a separate biographical page for the Walters man. He wasn't married but it showed that he had four children. But they only had the name of one son.

Kyron Grant.

A crippling light-headedness washed over me. My fingers began to tremble so fiercely that the sheet of paper almost slipped out of my hands. I gripped it more tightly, until my fingers dampened. Chills invaded my body like relentless soldiers, and I fought the urge to heave, standing right there in front of the copy machine.

What the hell?

Just four days ago, I was kissing Kyron, folding under his hands. We'd stayed out by the pool, talking for hours until his cousin began blowing up his phone. He listened patiently as I shared how resolute I was in moving forward with my Georgetown application and how petrified I became every time I thought about losing my parents' support. And the way he looked at me all throughout the night, in those pajamas and that raggedy ponytail, like he wouldn't trade positions with any other guy, anywhere. Since that night, Kyron had invaded my thoughts like nothing else had. And today I was holding a revelation that wedged between us like a brick wall.

I grabbed the pile of papers and returned to my desk, not wanting to know the additional details of the case, and at the same time, needing to torture myself with the information. I pored over the file at breakneck speed, gliding over the lines so I got the gist of the details but not lingering too long for fear of being consumed by them. From what the detectives had gleaned so far, Anderson had been skimming off the top of the money he dropped off each month for Kyron and his mother. When it got back to Grafton Walters, he apparently gave Anderson an opportunity to pay back a portion of the money. Or work it off. But Anderson had denied the accusations. His body parts were found the next day. And Grafton Walters seemed to have covered the tracks of the hitmen involved.

My head was on the brink of imploding. My father had polished and buffed his image for public consumption, packaged and presented his family as the honourable and respectable choice. An affiliation like this could torpedo his campaign. In as much as everybody talked about my rebellious streak, could I really betray my own? That scheming user was my flesh and blood. And yet, the thought of losing Kyron made a strangled, frustrated cry escape my throat. I pinched my eyes together with my fingers and then reached for my phone to text Kyron.

> ME: You there?

His reply came almost immediately.

> KYRON: Hey Chels. Was just gonna call you to ask if you wanna go see a movie when you done over there.

> ME: You had any plans of telling me that Grafton Walters is your father?

It was a little too late for formalities. I saw the dialogue bubbles form, and then disappear. And then they formed again.

> Kyron: Chelsea, he is a non-issue. You, more than anybody else, know he not a part of my life.

Was he serious?

> ME: If he's so much of a non-issue, why keep that information from me?

KYRON: Because I wanted to have a chance with you!

My mind was warring. How did Kyron not see that keeping this from me reeked of manipulation? The Kyron I had come to know over the last few weeks respected me enough to not want to control me. That Kyron would have disclosed this information to me, respecting my ability to come to my own decision.

KYRON: Chels, I am not him…

ME: I know, but

If our worlds were far apart before this information was revealed, there was practically a gaping chasm between them now.

KYRON: But what Chels? You worried about what your parents will think? Still?

Oddly enough, I wasn't. My parents' opinions hadn't actually crossed my mind. But I did understand the entirety of who I was, including my place in the family to which I was born.

ME: This isn't about my parents.

KYRON: Exactly. It's about you! Your life and what you want.

ME: Yeah, we agree on that. I get to choose. So the answer is no. We can't do this Kyron. You know that as well as I do.

KYRON: Chelsea, I was going to tell you. But I kept picturing this exact conversation we having now! And I just wasn't ready for that.

ME: You can't help who your father is. I get that. But neither can I.

My phone sat in my lap for so long that I almost thought he wasn't going to respond. I knew the emotions loaded behind that silence because I felt them too. And then he typed.

KYRON: Chels.

I answered him before he seized the opportunity to send another text.

ME: Delete my number Kyron. Please.

* * *

KYRON

The rift between Chelsea and me grew over the next few days, with barely any words exchanged between us. It was so crazy to think that just the week before, I was kissing her, feeling confident about her wanting to be with me. Thinking about what it would be like to have her as my girlfriend and how I was going to put it in place. The texts I sent to her either went unanswered or were met with distant responses that almost diminished the significance of the amount of time we'd spent together. Compared to that, I preferred to have no communication with her at all. So I hadn't contacted her in the last three days. Every time I reached for the phone, I talked myself into putting it down. Today, she still sat next to me in class but there was no smile at me from the corner of her mouth. She didn't say a word. After wavering back and forth, I scrawled some words on a notebook page and slipped it to her.

I'm sorry.

To my relief, she didn't scowl, or worse, rip it up and fling the pieces into the air. But a look of disappointment came over her face, and knowing that I was responsible for that look made me wish that she'd just gotten angry instead. I felt like I'd been cuffed in the stomach. Chelsea had trusted me enough with her fears and how she loathed the way her parents attempted to rule her life. But in some crazy way, in withholding information from her, I had done the same thing. I hadn't trusted her to come to a decision on us with all the facts, even the ugly ones. I exhaled a thankful breath when I saw her writing something in return. She passed it to me and our fingers brushed, reminding me of the few times I'd gotten to hold her.

Me too.

Just then, Mrs. Cross did her customary dismissal, warning us that the weeks were dwindling and we needed to be more conscientious of our work as the time drew nearer. I was sure that Chelsea could sense me walking behind her. As soon as we were outside in the hallway, I took her hand, surprising her.

If she was ending this, I had to hear her say those words, and there needed to be some kind of certainty there. I led her down a corridor, close to the doors of the auditorium. I found a corner next to a window, hidden from view.

I waited for her to face me but she was avoiding my eyes in a way that was so uncharacteristic, I became frustrated. I tipped her chin up and even then, she wouldn't focus on me.

"Look at me, Chels."

She licked her lips but still wouldn't meet my eyes. I didn't want to push her but I needed to get through to her somehow. So I lowered my head until we were face to face. So that she didn't have a choice but to see me. How was it that I was so stressed about losing her and she wasn't even mine to lose?

"I'm sorry I didn't say anything." I couldn't believe how much emotion was clogging my damn throat. "I should've trusted you with that information. I couldn't deal with the thought of you not wanting to have anything to do with me."

Her eyes didn't look affected. She didn't look repulsed but she didn't look forgiving. There was just an empty stare on her usually expressive face. I'd seen her give that look to other people, so it hurt like hell to now be on the receiving end of it.

"Chelsea, if we want to be together, this wouldn't affect that. I promise I'll never keep anything from you again."

"Don't make promises you can't keep," she warned. "You don't get it, Kyron – it's more than the manipulation."

"Well explain it to me," I urged desperately, holding on to both her hands now.

She sighed heavily. "I can forgive you for not telling me about your father. I already have. But I can't bring this kind of scrutiny on mine. He doesn't deserve that."

The tension mounting in me by the second, I released her and dragged my hand over my face.

"Do you know that as of Monday he's projected to win by five seats?" she asked, her voice laced with resignation. "In the papers they saying that the election swung in his favour the moment I came off that stage Saturday," she added, smirking drily.

"I only got to go on that date with you because I promised my father I'd do that address in Tobago. Now that same speech likely gonna win him the election."

Damn.

"I can't put him at risk like that, Kyron," she said, compelling me to see the situation from her perspective. "He's worked too hard. I can't do that to him now, and I sure as hell can't do it to him when he's the Prime Minister."

And I knew I couldn't realistically expect her to.

"The sins of the father," I mumbled.

Her responding exhale was long and just as tortured as I felt.

This – the collateral consequence of being born to a particular lineage – was a battle I knew all about, because I was fighting it myself. I couldn't change whose blood ran through my veins just as much as she couldn't change hers. Without even realizing what I was doing, I curled my hand around Chelsea's neck one last time, as I had done when I'd experienced the best kiss of my life. I breathed in her vanilla scent, committing it to memory. And then, I kissed her forehead and walked away.

* * *

CHELSEA

The drive from The Centre to Gasparillo was a painfully long, emotional upheaval. Traffic lights took too long to change and cars in front of us were practically crawling. Pedestrians lingered too long in crosswalks and I'd never known the Benz to drive so slowly.

When Carlisle dropped me off in front of Gramma's house, I was in a daze. My insides felt like someone had gutted them out with an ice-scream scoop. Having Kyron kiss my head, with such tenderness and reverence, was the most achingly painful thing I had ever felt. Neighbour Harold and Tanty Jean were both rocking in their gallery, bright smiles on their faces. I waved to them and hurried inside, certain that if I delayed too long I wouldn't be able to fend off the threatening tears.

When I got to Gramma's kitchen, I saw her bent over the stove, tasting some soup with a pot spoon. It wasn't Saturday if she didn't make cow-heel soup. And normally, that broth could cure any ailment. I was less faithful today. Unable to offer any kind of greeting, I lay my head on the table. And then, the dam broke. I wasn't even sure why I was crying. I felt like an aching hole sat at my core, filled only with the loss of the most special guy I had ever met. I didn't even want to think about what my days would look like now, without his smile, or his jokes, or his touch.

My grandmother came over to me, sitting in the chair next

to mine. She didn't speak, just passed her hand over my back, soothingly.

"Alright, dahlin. Alright," she said, after some time.

No words would come, just sobs.

"Nothing wrong with a good cry. If anybody say otherwise, tell dem come check your grandmother. You hear meh?"

"Yes, Gramma," I said, as she gathered me in her arms. My tears soaked the front of her duster but her hand remained on my head, calming me in that way that only she could. She rocked me gently, crooning in my ear, off-key as usual.

What a friend we have in Jesus;
All our sins and griefs to bear.
What a privilege to carry;
Everything to God in prayer.

She sang that chorus three times before my tears eventually subsided. I didn't exactly think God had the time to spare on a teenager's love life but I didn't voice my doubts in this regard. Gramma sounded sure, and that was enough to ease my anxiety. I sat upright, prepared for her questioning but uncertain how I would answer. When I looked at her though, I didn't see interrogation. Only kindness. I did not, and would not, ever understand what I had done to deserve Eloise Marchand. The fact that she was even a part of my world was humbling.

"Gramma –"

"Hush, meh chile," she said, cutting me off. "I know the way Carlisle does be running up and down with you, you eh put nothing hot on your stomach for the morning yet. Come, let meh dish out some soup for you."

I had no words for that invitation, only an acquiescing nod

of the head.

* * *

KYRON

As soon as I left The Centre, I jumped into my car and flew down the highway towards Point Lisas. I hardly remembered the drive there, my mind bombarded by the image of Chelsea's face as I walked away from her. I barged through the factory doors without permission, propelled by the rage that crept up my spine. A few workers were operating their machines, and they looked up, stunned, as I charged to the back. I only vaguely heard Gary calling out to me in the distance, warning me that my father was busy. My thoughts flashed to when I came here to confront him about Anderson. My discomfiture that night contrasted starkly to how impetuous I felt now.

By the time I got to his office, my veins were straining and pulsing against my skin. His gaze found mine, his hard, flinty eyes matching my own.

"I thought you say what you do in your life doh affect me?" I asked him bitterly. "Well it sure as hell doh seem so!"

My father crossed his arms and leisurely ran his right hand over his chin. He bared his teeth but remained silent, which only made my blood burn.

"I doh understand how a man who was never there for me,

not one day ... a man who never step a foot in my mother house ... could plague my life."

He still refused to speak.

"And I here like a jackass, walking 'round thinking I could live free and clear of you. Hell, I doh even have your last name!"

My father leaned back in his chair and propped both his feet on the corner of his desk.

"How you feel to know I finally get a girl I really care for ... a girl from a good family. The Marchand family of all people! And the only thing preventing us from being together is you! I couldn't even be upfront about who my own father is. Dat seem fair to you?"

I was heaving so much my throat was growing dry. And still, my father said nothing. His composure made me want to explode.

"Answer meh!" I shouted, slamming both hands on his desk so hard the stack of pens on top of it toppled over.

And then he began to speak, his tone admonishing, his words deliberate.

"Fair? You wanna know what's not fair, Kyron? Not knowing the truth, son." He gave a harsh, steely laugh. "The way I see it, the next Prime Minister of Trinidad and Tobago shouldn't take any issue with you dating his daughter. None at all."

My forehead creased. What was that even supposed to mean? This man and his damn mind games and riddles. As he stared at me impassively, I knew my ranting would have no effect on him. That his usual stoicism would only aggravate me more than I already was. I turned to walk away but his even voice stopped me mid-stride.

"Marchand was my accountant back in the day. You think your father alone have sins to atone for?" He scoffed. "You find Marchand and he family could just sit down in their ivory tower while you demonize me? Eh?"

I was tempted to turn around but something about his tone glued me to where I stood, had my mind racing with the implication of his words.

"That's not what I meant."

"Like hell it wasn't." There was a gruffness to his tone I'd never heard before.

I swallowed over the tightness in my throat and glanced at him from my periphery, absorbing his derisive expression.

"If you hold de next first family in such high regard, if you speak of them in these lofty terms ... well, let's just hope you never find out what Marchand hired me to do when his business partner was going to blow his whole operation."

Chapter 11

CHELSEA

The night before election day, I entered my house to the unusual sound of my parents arguing. My mother believed that quarrelling wasn't ladylike so she never engaged in it. I dropped my bag in the living room and headed to my bedroom, from where I could hear the intensity of elevated voices.

When I reached the door, I saw my father standing with my SAT maths textbook in one hand and a pamphlet for the Georgetown Writers' Corner in the next. My mother looked exasperated by her inability to explain my defiance to him. I yearned to tell her she need not find the words. That I was fully capable of defending myself. And more than that, I was eager to. I'd done my part in their charade. Performed loyally as was expected of me. Stayed away from the guy I went to bed thinking about every night. Tomorrow, the voters were headed to the polling booths to choose my father. I had my own choices to make.

"You want to explain this?" Daddy asked, holding up the book. His chilled tone would have been disconcerting, had I not been his daughter.

"No. But I will. I'm taking the SAT exam in a few weeks," I said, dividing my attention between them both, my arms crossed over my chest.

"SAT?" My mother pressed. "Chelsea, why are you doing this? We've already discussed that you're going to England."

"We discussed it? Or both of you demanded it?"

My father began yelling. "You mean to tell me after all I and your mother sacrifice, you going and traipse off to dat God-forsaken country? To do what, Chelsea? To write what?" His thundering voice bounced off all four walls of my room.

My patience, already waning, snapped like a fragile twig. It could have been the incredulity in the pounding rhythm of his words. Or maybe it was finally realizing that while I was so concerned about preserving his appearance, protecting his dream, he couldn't care less about mine.

"Who exactly the sacrifice was for, Daddy? When you change the Trust to keep your hand like a noose around meh neck! When you send meh to go prying for information for this damn election! Who was all that for? Me or you? Tell meh!"

My mother stood to the side of the bed, her mouth ajar and her face struck with horror. Heat travelled the length of my body. I crept closer to where they stood, until there was a barely a breath of space between the sharp angles of my father's face and the tremors of my own. I wasn't sure if I was shaking with rage or terror.

"You eh find you use meh enough?" I ground out. "You don't think me and Mummy was sacrificing when the police came here, breaking down the door looking for you after Mr. Lezama had get kill? When I had to watch Mummy lie to them?"

My mother whimpered beside me. I observed my father's bulging eyes and became convinced that if this conversation continued along these lines for two more minutes, he'd burst a blood vessel.

"Lydia, you see these games this child playin'?"

And then he faced me, squaring himself. My tears were building, scorching until it felt like my eyes were on fire. As my frame began to shrink, I steeled myself, readying for his accusations, his attacks. He didn't speak at first. Just puffed noisily from his chest.

"If you feel I going and stand up here and allow my child, the child that I make, the child who back I put clothes on, to talk to me like that, you lie."

I blinked back the burning liquid behind my eyelids as my father slammed the door behind me.

* * *

KYRON

After football, I was skimming my timeline when I saw a video of Marchand's victory speech at the ANP headquarters. His Cabinet ministers all stood behind him, bouncing up and down with the excitement of the win. Chelsea and her mother flanked him on each side, the pride shining on their faces. Something about that video crystallized it for me. That her father was going to be running the country. Madness.

I was staring at her. Even with a grainy cell phone video, I'd fallen right back into the habit. Her smile was kinda stiff though. A little forced. She was still showing everything on her face. Frustrated, I shoved my phone into my pocket and jumped into the car.

When I pulled up in front the house, I saw a black Range Rover parked by the fence. I'd never seen that van before but my suspicion regarding its owner was enough to raise the hairs on my arm. I delayed every action that would bring me closer to seeing him. Parking the car and closing the gate. Grabbing my cleats and the small bag of groceries Ma had asked that I pick up. Even my approach to the door was deliberate, lingering on each step.

"Goodnight," I greeted as I edged in.

"Goodnight, Kyron," came his booming voice, in chorus with my mother's lighter one.

She was in the armchair, not far from where she'd been

keeled over bawling her guts out over Anderson. Her eyes were shifty, expectant. As if she was unsure how I'd react to this scene. And my father was sitting on the couch, looking out of place in a suit. I'd never seen him in this house. Couldn't recall the last time he'd even stopped by our gap. His money had repaired the floors I was standing on. He'd literally put this roof over my head. But he'd never stepped under it. Yet here he was, reaching to an end table for a glass of juice that sat on a napkin, signalling his presence here as that of a guest. Whether he was an unwelcome one from my mother's perspective, I didn't know.

"What you doing here?" I was more curious than anything but there was an acidity in my tone that I couldn't conceal.

My father's jaw jutted out. With his elbows on his knees, his hands hung between his legs.

"A sad day when a father hears his son ask why he's in his presence."

"Nah, we eh doing that victim thing today. You not going to turn this on me. Not in this house," I warned, tossing my shoes in a corner and putting the bag of groceries on the living room table.

He cracked a cutting smile. "Well, in any event, I won't burden you too much longer. On my way to a meeting with our new Prime Minister."

I could feel my eyes bugging. "Meeting 'bout what?"

"Well, I'm sure you know how bad this violence is these days, Kyron. All these warring gangs. These young boys killing one another without remorse. I think he figures I can be some kind of community activist."

"Mmm, like talk some sense into them fellas," I finished

with scorn.

"Yeah, well, something like that. A little direction wouldn't hurt them. Do something enterprising with themselves. So they could take care of their families."

A bitterness was building in my mouth. His disclosure a few weeks back was still churning in my head. But I'd meant what I said to Chelsea. We could untangle ourselves from our parents. Their misdeeds didn't have a permanent place over our heads.

Ma spoke up from the corner. "But the main reason he wanted to pass was because I told him about your scholarship," she reassured.

"Yes, yes, very impressive accomplishment," he added. "I know that there will be a lot of logistics involved. Getting your student visa, booking your flight. There's a cost to these things. Just wanted to contribute in any way I could. Make this process a little less stressful."

He reached into the inside of his jacket and extended a swollen, white envelope to me. The way his hand was outstretched exposed a thick gold bracelet around his wrist. At my hesitation, there was insistence in his eyes, and he pushed the envelope further in my direction. I took it and peeled it open. My fingers curled around a thousand US dollars. There were only ten bills, so thin and crisp that they could have just come from the Mint. And still, the envelope had a kind of weight to it. A heaviness. One that I couldn't wait to get rid of any longer.

"Nah. I good," I said, walking to my mother and pressing it into her folded hands. And then I left for my bedroom, leaving the two of them where they sat.

* * *

CHELSEA

"You ready, sweetheart?"

"Gimme a few more minutes, Mummy. Just finishing this," I answered, peering closer at my laptop screen. Nothing needed to be fixed, really, but I was triple-checking the information I'd entered, obsessing over every word. Mummy floated into the room with her blue sun-dress and floppy white hat. You'd never tell we were headed for the same place, given that I was sitting at my desk in an ANP jersey and my underwear. Today was my father's victory motorcade. He clinched twenty-four out of the forty-one seats, as well as the majority vote. Normally, motorcades were held before the election. Trust Peter Marchand to be the anomaly.

At the last rally, a man had shouted from the front of the crowd during one of Daddy's infamous pauses.

"When is de motorcade?"

The air was already charged with a kind of premonitory euphoria, so his question had only amped up the crowd further, until they began chanting for an answer. Daddy held up his hands to simmer them down, and in smooth segue, responded, "I am not a man of premature celebrations, unlike my opponent, Roger Pierre. Someone who counts his chickens before they hatch isn't fit to lead a bachac to a leaf, much less the citizens of this beloved nation to a prosperous future."

They'd roared, duped and taken by him yet again. So today we were about to shake hands and wave to his supporters, across the East-West Corridor, in the blazing hot sun. With my mother looking like she was headed to a tea party. She glanced around my room with tartness and sat on the edge of the bed, then observed me as I worked on the computer. From the corner of my eye, I saw her examining my laptop screen.

There was a stutter on her lips so I pre-empted her question.

"Yes, Mummy. This is my Georgetown application."

I'd begun working on it after my parents had left my room that evening, and decided to apply for early admission. No sense waiting on my SAT scores when I'd already made up my mind. My mother cleared her throat.

"So, I take it you're doing this."

"Yes, Mummy."

I tried to ignore her presence and concentrate, proof-reading my personal statement for the hundredth time. In my mind, I'd planned a cultured, masterful essay meant to persuade them that I deserved a spot in the programme. But when I began typing, that idea soon morphed into an exposé. An unsanitized account of my journey to this point. From betrayal, to loss, to resolve. When I'd first read my words, it felt like I'd vomited on the page. They read too raw, too open. Too truthful to share with a panel of strangers. Especially the closing sentences.

For me, a seat in this class is a stand in my truth. Unmasked. Against my parents cautioning me that I'm out of position. And on the shoulders of a grandmother who's never doubted my unrepentance for yearning to do some fancy business with words.

What tore at me most was the ambivalence, the clashing feelings. What felt like a betrayal to my parents simultaneously felt like a really long exhale. So I'd read the statement three more times. Each time slower than the last. And, ultimately, resisted the urge to delete it.

I turned to face Mummy, absorbed the way her eyes overflowed with disappointment. Even with her customary rigid posture, her shoulders drooped.

"Why, Chelsea?"

That question left her lips like a plea, like a longing to understand a puzzle that was truly incomprehensible to her. You would think I wanted to hop on someone's pole. But in that moment, her disappointment couldn't even begin to rival my own. We were less than five minutes into this conversation and the frustration was already rising from my core, eating away at me.

"That's exactly what I should be asking you. I don't get it, Mummy," I urged, flinging my hands in the air. I went to my closet and pulled down a pair of jeans, shoving my legs into them.

"Daddy has an agenda. Fine. He never hides it from me, so I can manage his expectations. But why you not protecting me from that? Is years now I waiting for you to step in when he tries to dictate. To tell him that I get to choose my aspirations. That y'all raised me to have a mind of my own. Or pretended to, at least."

When she replied, her volume elevated but it didn't nearly match my own.

"What need is there for me to intervene, Chelsea? There is nothing more important to your father than your success."

"Because he's the one orchestrating it!" I practically shouted. "Is it really my success when he has me on this carefully designed journey? When every turn, every detour is his doing?"

My heart was hammering in my chest from the need for my mother to understand me. Did she really not get where I was coming from?

Her feet tapped my carpet and her head shook to either side.

"You have so much to be grateful for," she said.

I licked my lips and returned to my chair, plopping down on the seat.

"This is not about me being ungrateful for what you and Daddy provide. I don't take any of that for granted. I just need to find my own way. And I'm not asking you or Daddy to let me do it either."

"And who says that way can't be law school?"

Before I could hold my tongue, I blurted, "Mummy, if you think being a lawyer is so great, maybe you should go."

"I tried," she mumbled, diverting her eyes.

My jaw dropped. I considered her soft words, watched her fingers strum my bed sheet.

"What?"

The heat must have been getting to her because she removed her hat and set it on the bed. She looked unnerved, unprepared to delve deeper into this conversation. So I half expected her to give me some dismissive response.

"I said I tried to go. You know my background is business. And I loved it for so many years at the insurance company. I really did. But something inside me always gravitated towards law. In retrospect, I couldn't tell you what it was," she said, shrugging. "So years after I already left UWI, even though I was doing so well at the company, I decided to apply to do my first degree in law."

My mother's eyes shrank and there was a lull of silence in the room before she continued.

"I've told you before that your father and I met on UWI's campus."

"Right. He was a lecturer."

"Yeah, well, it was when I went to pick up the application. He was young but he was already starting to move and shake in politics and associate with so many big-name attorneys. It wasn't much long after your father and I married that we got pregnant with you. Now, don't get me wrong, darling. I love the life I chose," she assured me. "I ... I wanted to leave my job and watch you grow up. To help your father manoeuvre in these political circles. I enjoyed all of it. Still do."

"Yeah, you look like you do."

I didn't need the earnestness in her voice to reaffirm what she was saying. I'd never noticed discontentment in my mother. She'd always seemed happy tinkering in her garden in the back, playing hostess on weekends, donning expensive dresses and being draped on my father's arm as they went to galas. Her tinkling laughter at the functions I'd attended with them never seemed forced. And in the last few months, she seemed to truly enjoy her role as part of Daddy's campaign strategy. This was just who she was. But now, as I bent forward in my chair, really studying her, I noticed the tinge of regret in the creases at the corner of her eyes and above her lips.

"In as much as I cherish the life I lead, I do wonder sometimes," she mumbled, leaning back on her arms. "Every now and again, I think that the dream hasn't gone away. That it's still buried somewhere inside. So when I see your father pushing you in the direction I wanted for myself, I stand back. Hoping you'll achieve what I didn't."

"I won't," I told her. "I shouldn't have to."

"Yeah, well, I see that now," she said, chuckling and wiping at the corner of her eye. She didn't look relieved. Or apologetic. Her expression was resigned more than anything else. Like she was just tired. And then her eyes softened.

"I guess being his speechwriter isn't out of the question, right?" she asked. Before I responded, Daddy's figure zoomed past. He must have glimpsed us because he backtracked and stood at the door.

"So allyuh in here having a pow-pow? Time to go up the road," he said, rolling up the sleeves of his ANP shirt. He was wearing khakis and a fedora. At the sight of him, Mummy fluffed her hair, picked up her hat and adjusted it on her head.

"Y'all ready?" Daddy asked.

"One second," I said, swivelling on my chair. I gave my application one final glance. Then I clicked the 'submit' button, sending it into a blackhole. When I turned around, both my parents were at the foot of my bed. My father's eyes were narrowed, sceptical slits. And my mother smoothed the skirt of her dress, bowing her head in an attempt to hide her smile.

"Yeah, I'm ready now."

Daddy began to respond but was interrupted by the shrill

sound of the house phone downstairs. At first, all three of us remained still. Then I sprang to my feet to catch the phone before the caller hung up.

I picked up the receiver to hear a panicky Shelly-Ann on the line.

"Chelsea! Chelsea!" came her urgent breaths. My pulse sped up and I almost dropped the phone.

"Shelly-Ann, what going on?"

"Come down the road quick," she practically bawled. "Gramma fall down in the bathroom and hit her head. She not breathing."

My world rocked and spun off its axis. Unable to bear my weight any longer, my knees buckled until I sank to the ground. My breath was coming in gasps, heaving in and out of my body. And then I heard Shelly-Ann's strangled cry on the other end of the line.

"Grammaaaa!"

Chapter 12

CHELSEA

Mount Sinai Baptist Church was a modest, flat concrete building, with too few windows. White standing fans were placed in each corner of the room to oscillate. A small altar at the front of the church was covered with lit candles and some of the same brass bowls that I had seen in my grandmother's home. There were about ten pews in all, with uncoordinated wooden benches. The large church doors were closed. Only Shelly-Ann, my parents and I were inside the building, as it was custom here for the family to view the body privately before the service began.

Not Gramma. The body.

She certainly looked like Gramma, with her head-tie wrapped intricately, and flowing church gown belted at the waist. But her essence had already left. That thing inside of her that reached out and cradled me when I needed her. And I just knew that that essence must have gone somewhere, because it was too big, and too potent to just disappear into nothingness. Shelly-Ann and I stood side by side at the coffin, staring at her. I told myself to move away, to start thinking about how to face overwhelming days and uncertain nights without her. Shelly-Ann dabbed her eyes with a handkerchief, whispering sweet words to her. Thanking her for loving her. Asking her why she had to leave. And I debated the wisdom of prying myself out of the numbness and leaning into the grief. That internal struggle was no use though, as I could already feel the sobs rising in my throat.

My father joined us with measured, heavy steps. There was anguish in his gait. His mouth was downturned and his shoulders were pulled low. Mummy went to his side and took his hand. And then a one-sided conversation unfolded, the likes of which I had never heard before.

"You was the best person I knew, Mammy. I was nothing like you," he said, with a brusque laugh.

I suddenly realized that I didn't recognize this man, as he was so different from the one who had been commanding audiences for so many nights during the preceding months. The man at the coffin was tentative, faltering and almost ... penitent.

"Ah didn't deserve you, Mammy. So ahh ... I glad that the big man upstairs lent you to me."

He stalled then, opening his mouth and closing it again, looking like he was at a loss for the right words.

"Rice, flour, sugar, oil and the gift of a new day. That was always enough for you." In all the years of knowing him, I had never seen my father look so haunted.

"I didn't learn much from you. You try your best, but my head was hard like banga. Even as a grown man. We didn't have a lot growing up and you know that used to bother me real plenty. I used to feel like if I just did things a certain way, I would always have." Daddy dropped his chin to his chest.

And then he covered his eyes with one hand and laid the other against his breastbone.

"I could never be the man you want me to be, Mammy. Ah try. Ah sorry eh. Ah sorry eh, Mammy." His voice broke in a way that broke me in turn. Water filled his blood-red eyes until it spilled over the rims. And then his voice lost its power. His next words were so soft I barely heard them. In that instant, it was as if he and his mother were all alone in the church.

"But you know what, Mammy? I know what I didn't take, Chelsea take. So ah thank you for that. For being there for meh daughter."

Just then, the pastor exited from the back room, looking sheepish at interrupting. He asked us if we were ready for the service to begin. We gave him the go-ahead and took our seats on the front bench.

Shortly afterwards, the church filled to capacity. There were wooden chairs outside the door, under a tent, to accommodate more people. Before the service began, the Pastor reminded everyone in attendance that Mother Eloise was the perennial joyful woman. That she came into the doors of the church singing. She didn't need music. She didn't even need the correct words for the song. He told us not to feel shame if we couldn't hold a tune; Gramma never cared that she was off-key anyway. His narrative paved the way for joyous singing, clapping and beating of drums. They danced around that church, swaying and stomping their feet and shouting so much I forgot, even if momentarily, that this was the funeral of the woman I considered my lifeline.

About half an hour into the service, the Pastor looked to me for some kind of signal of my readiness. I nodded.

Daddy had sent his lawyer to Gramma's house a few years ago to organize her affairs. Apparently, she had fussed and carried on, claiming that she wasn't going in the ground with anything, so he could tell my father to do with her possessions as he pleased. At the lawyer's insistence, Gramma had managed to come up with three requests before offering him a plate of oil down and a cold glass of lime juice. She'd told him that she wanted me to be the beneficiary of her small life-insurance policy, that Shelly-Ann was to get the house, and that I would give her eulogy, minus all them fancy words I liked to use.

Shelly-Ann squeezed my hand in encouragement and my mother offered one of her contained smiles. I was ready though. I gathered my dress, went up to the pulpit, and unfolded my crumpled up piece of paper. The crowd looked even larger than it did while I was sitting in the pew, and standing up there felt vaguely reminiscent of giving the speech in Tobago. Today though, I would address the small gathering on my own terms. As my grandmother had long instructed. As she had dreamed.

With a deep breath, I began to speak.

"Afternoon, church."

"Afternoon," they chorused.

"Eloise Marchand was my everything. My strength, my restoration, and my hope. So as you can imagine, it's been unfortunate for me that she's been ready to meet Jesus for as long as I've been alive," I said, with a wobbly smile. "But that was the thing about that woman. She was like that because her God was her source. Her faith was her everything. She didn't need anyone to validate her. She didn't seek anyone's approval. And she surely didn't need anyone's permission to live the life that she wanted to live."

My heart cracked straight down the centre. I stood on the shore. She sat in the boat. But I didn't know who was leaving whom. I wasn't sure it mattered, really. I felt my spine straightening, and my breathing level and normalize.

"And that's what she wanted for me. That was her dream. All that I found in her, she wanted me to find in myself. Knowing that I already had it in me."

I didn't look at my parents while I was speaking. My eyes never fell on Shelly-Ann. And it took everything in me not to look down at the coffin where my grandmother slept. But, I managed. I focused my gaze straight ahead – past the familiar faces I saw in the crowd, straight out the front of the church to where the sun was beating down mercilessly on the concrete pathway.

"Today, there is so much to thank her for. I could stand up here all day and speak about what a magnificent, wonderful light she was. But more than anything else, I thank her for passing on to me what she knew. For teaching me. For showing me."

"Thank you, Father!" came an approving shout from someone outside under the tent.

I looked down at my paper and realized that I hadn't said anything that I had planned on saying. On that paper were words unspoken, and surprisingly, no tears.

"I thought I'd end by asking everyone to join me in singing one of her favourite hymns. 'When We All Get to Heaven'."

I stepped down from the podium and Shelly-Ann reached out to hug me, as the church filled with voices so loud that the building almost shook with their fervour.

When the service was over, Shelly-Ann and I gathered the brightly coloured wreaths that friends had brought, and placed them in the car. Daddy, Carlisle and the other pallbearers came out the church with careful steps and positioned the coffin to place it in the hearse. With my hand on my forehead, shading my eyes from the sun, I watched as the hearse drove down the street, taking away my grandmother.

And then I noticed Kyron standing in front his car, dressed in dark blue dress pants, and a blue and white striped dress shirt. He had just opened the door for a woman whom I assumed was his mother. My eyes met his. I saw hesitation in them. As I crossed the street to head towards him, his face was the embodiment of sheer surprise. I didn't blame him. We hadn't exchanged a word since the Saturday he'd kissed my forehead and walked away. Since I'd pushed him away.

When I got to him, we both hovered in each other's presence for a while, unsure yet eager. And then I made the first move, extending my arms over his shoulders. He wrapped me in a hug that felt better than any I'd ever experienced. I had managed to remain composed during the eulogy, but now I dissolved into a teary mess right there in his arms. I didn't know how he got here. I had no idea who told him or who gave him directions. But I was glad he was here. I clung to him as if dozens of church people weren't watching, and his arms were around my back like he didn't care either. My body began to quake in his embrace, with both grief and gratitude.

"It's okay, Chels," he said in my ear comfortingly, planting a soft kiss on the side of my head. It was only when my body stopped shaking that I leaned away from him. He reached for a handkerchief from his pocket and dried a few of my tears before handing it to me.

"How you find out?"

"Saw it on the news a few nights ago."

"Well I appreciate that you here. It's a ... very pleasant surprise."

Kyron just shrugged like it was nothing to him.

"Grams didn't know me from Adam when she interceded on my behalf like I was her own grandchild. Plus, in that same phone call she told me about how important it is to show my face at a time like this. Sooo, this is me showing my face."

I remembered. And I recalled how it didn't take more than Gramma saying that for him to head to Anderson's wake.

"Yeah, she was that kind of special."

"And she has a special granddaughter too," he said, almost bashfully, lowering his gaze.

I didn't know how to respond to that, and since Kyron and I did silence so well, even strained silence, I said nothing at all.

"Very nice eulogy by the way. I sure she thought it was

perfect."

"Yeah, I tried to do her proud. No big words for her to complain about."

"And you meant all dem things you said? Fight the power?" he asked.

I gave a long, deep exhale, considering a fitting answer.

"Well, I guess that's left to be seen, right? I'm gonna have to prove it to myself."

The smile he gave me almost melted my insides.

"Yeah, I guess so."

There was so much that needed to be said between us. So much I still had to disclose. He'd sounded so sure when he said the two of us could just be. Despite everything. And everyone.

"Is that your mother in the car?" I asked.

"Yeah," he said, rubbing the back of his neck. "We were just about to head to the cemetery."

"Chelsea," my father called out to me. I hadn't realized that Carlisle had pulled the car around. I saw my mother seated in the back, composed as usual. My father sat next to her, holding the door open for me. "Come on," Daddy said. "We headed down now. Jump in."

I walked over to the car, closed the door, and kissed his cheek through the window.

"I getting a ride with Kyron, so I'll see you guys when I reach."

When I caught Carlisle's eye in the side mirror, I could see him smothering a smile, and before my father got the opportunity to even form a discernable expression, Carlisle let up off the brakes and drove my parents out onto the main road. I turned to see that Kyron hadn't moved. His mother was looking at us through the windshield, her face alight with undisguised curiosity.

I didn't even realize I was tapping my nose until Kyron addressed me, his eyes focusing on me with an intensity unmatched by any other time I'd caught him looking at me before.

"Wah goin through your mind?" he asked.

"Just wondering how your mother would react if you introduced me as your girlfriend," I said uncertainly. I didn't know where I stood with Kyron, or if he even wanted to be with me after the way the last few weeks had unfolded. In that moment, I only knew that I wanted to be in his messy world, and I needed for him to be a part of my chaotic one. A flash of astonishment passed across his face, giving way to a pensive appearance that told of his turning over something in his head. I knew that look well. Then, an achingly slow and tender smile crept across his face, lighting up his features in a way that made something inside me lift.

"Well, we goin' and find out."

THE END

ABOUT THE AUTHOR

Between growing up in Trinidad and Tobago and living in the United States, Tamika has always been observing the rich stories unfolding around her. She first attempted novel writing when she was twelve years old, penning a young adult story in two notebooks that she stuck together by the covers with glue. Tamika was first published in *The Caribbean Writer* with her short story entitled *A Christmas Eve Wedding*. She holds an English degree from Morgan State University and enjoys writing almost as much as she loves reading. *Dreams Beyond the Shore* is her first published novel.

TALES FOR YOUNG ADULTS
FROM BLOUSE & SKIRT BOOKS

ALL OVER AGAIN
BY A-DZIKO SIMBA GEGELE
Who Knew Growing up
Could be so Hard?

GROWING UP IS HARD.
You know this. And when your mother has X-ray eyes and dances like a wobbling bag of water? When your father's idea of fun is to put all your money in a savings account and make you get up at 5 am every Sunday morning? When Kenny, Percival Thorton High's big show-off, is after Christina Parker – your Christina Parker? And when you have a shrimp of a little sister who is the bawlingest little six year old girl in the whole of Riverland? Then growing up is something you not sure you can manage at all. Who in their right mind could? Who? You?

All Over Again is an enchanting slice of boyhood. It is a charming coming of age story with a bold narrative style that pulls you into it.

Winner of the 2014 Burt Award for Caribbean Literature and longlisted for the 2015 International IMPAC Dublin Literary Award.

TALES FOR YOUNG ADULTS
FROM BLOUSE & SKIRT BOOKS

CHILDREN OF THE SPIDER
BY IMAM BAKSH
The Spiders are Coming!

MAYALI IS A GIRL on the run. Driven by desperation and the search for her father, Mayali leaves behind everything she has ever known on her home world of Zolpash, a land of sulphur and harsh weather, and journeys to Guyana. There she meets Joseph, a boy without the gift of speech but with much to say. Together they go on a daring, cross-country adventure to save earth from the invading Spider gods and their armies. Will their warning come too late? Will anyone even believe them? And will Mayali be able to find her father?

Children of the Spider is a fast-paced adventure. The story moves from the lush hinterlands of Guyana through to the bustling city of Georgetown where the colonial past continues to rub shoulders with the gritty, contemporary world. It is a refreshing take on Caribbean myth and mythology from an interesting new voice.

Children of the Spider won first place in the 2015 Burt Award for Caribbean Literature.

TALES FOR YOUNG ADULTS
FROM BLOUSE & SKIRT BOOKS

DANCING IN THE RAIN
BY LYNN JOSEPH
Finding Joy in the Small Things

TWELVE YEAR-OLD ELIZABETH is no normal girl. With an imagination that makes room for mermaids and magic in everyday life, she lives every moment to the fullest. Yet her joyful world crumbles around her when two planes bring down the Twin Towers and tear her family apart. Thousands of miles away, yet still touched by this tragedy, Elizabeth is swimming in a sea of loss. She finally finds hope when she meets her kindred spirit in 8 year-old Brandt and his 13 year-old brother, Jared.

Brandt and Jared, two boys as different as Oreo and milk and just as inseparable, arrive on the island to escape the mushroom of sorrow that bloomed above their lives in the wake of the tragedy. Elizabeth shows them a new way to look at the world and they help her to laugh again. But can Elizabeth and Brandt help their families see that when life brings showers of sadness, it's okay to dance in the rain?

Set against the dazzling beauty of the Dominican Republic, Dancing in the Rain explores the impact of the tragic fall of the Twin Towers on two Caribbean families. It is a lyrical, well-crafted tale about finding joy in the face of loss.

Dancing in the Rain won a Burt Award for Caribbean Literature (2015) prize.

TALES FOR YOUNG ADULTS
FROM BLOUSE & SKIRT BOOKS

GIRLCOTT
BY FLORENZ
WEBBE MAXWELL

EVEN IN PARADISE revolutions can be inconvenient things.

A week ago, Desma Johnson had only two things on her mind – in exactly eight days, she would be sixteen years old and to top it off she was inline for a top scholarship, bringing her one step closer to her dreams. Life was perfect and nothing would get in the way of her birthday plans. But it's 1959 and the secret Progressive League has just announced a boycott of all cinemas in Bermuda in order to end racial segregation.

As anxieties around the boycott build Desma becomes increasingly aware of the racial tensions casting a dire shadow over the island. Neighbours she once thought were friendly and supportive show another side. So, Desma must learn that change is never easy, and even when others expect small things from black girls, she has the right to dream big.

In this startling debut, Florenz Webbe Maxwell takes a little known fact about Caribbean history and weaves an engaging tale that speaks eloquently to the contemporary experience. Girlcott takes you beyond the image of Bermuda as a piece of paradise and charts a narrative of resistance, hope and the importance of fighting for change.

Girlcott won a Burt Award for Caribbean Literature (2016) prize.